# Endure

# Endure

A NOVEL *by*

TOSHIKO SHOJI ITO

BEAR
RIVER
PRESS

ISBN 0-9768528-0-2 (hardcover)
ISBN 0-9768528-1-0 (paperback)

Cover photo: *Foundation,* Minidoka Internment Center, Idaho
Photo copyright © 2001 by Emily Hanako Momohara

Book design by Roseline Seng
Text set in Sabon and News Gothic

Printed in the United States of America
2 4 6 8 9 7 5 3 1

Published by
BEAR RIVER PRESS
P.O. Box 1024
Torrance, CA 90505-0024

bearriverpress.com
(213)713-4975
(213)232-3317 fax
bearriver@verizon.net

*Loads of luck to a swell girl.*

—MINIDOKA, 1943

# Foreword

by Emily Hanako Momohara

Growing up as a *hapa* (half-Asian) American, I learned from my parents that my Japanese heritage was a source of pride. However, the window to my family's past remains sealed with shame. Much of the silence stems from the racism against—and incarceration of —the entire West Coast Japanese American community (120,000 people) during World War II. Seventy percent of those imprisoned were American citizens, born in the United States. Painful memories make it difficult for former internees to discuss their experience. Embarrassment from the false guilt put on them, by the government and society, has silenced my community's stories.

The author, Toshiko Shoji Ito, and my grandmother, Kiyomi (Doi) Momohara, were teenagers when they were sent to Minidoka Relocation Center in 1942. They both grew up in Seattle's *Nihonmachi* and both of their brothers volunteered for the U.S. Army and ended up in the 442nd Regimental Combat Team, an all-Japanese American unit. My grandmother and Ms. Ito also share the discomfort of discussing the circumstances surrounding Minidoka life. The similarities between these two women amazed me.

This book, although fictional, sheds light on their historical experiences seen through the eyes of a 17-year-old girl. I wish that it had been available for me when I was a teenager.

Ms. Ito's account of camp life, specifically the varying attitudes of those interned, is honest and insightful. She tries to convey all the different views that Japanese Americans and their Caucasian counterparts took toward each other. Sometimes relationships grew stronger, but mostly not. *Nikkei* (Japanese Americans) were also branded by each other, depending on their views about internment, the loyalty questionnaire, the draft, the resisters, and the "no-no" boys. Even though the community is still divided on these issues, learning about each person's convictions only makes me more proud of my Japanese American heritage. I have come to terms with the fact that none of them were wrong in their varying choices or opinions. The welfare of the family and the group as a whole was a concern of everyone's. However, each person chose a different way of expressing that passionate view.

I decided to dedicate my artistic endeavors to issues surrounding the internment and their effect on the younger generations. My grandmother's experience in camp and my desire for that story to be told led me to create a body of images taken from the internment camps. The photograph on the cover of this book is an homage to my grandmother. She is the foundation that supports my family and the unyielding stake that holds up the home. She did not teach

us to distrust the government, but encouraged her children and grandchildren to live the American dream. During the summer, she would watch me when my mother was at work. I remember her teaching me how to make *musubi* (rice balls) and taking me to *Obon odori* (Japanese dance) practice. But we also went to sporting events, waited in line for the latest delivery of Cabbage Patch Kids, and ate Hostess cupcakes while watching TV. In hindsight, I see that she was teaching me how to be a multicultural person, or more importantly, to enjoy my American life and Japanese culture. Today, I still stand on her strong foundation of hope, strength and *gaman* (endurance) that continues to support me as I grow in life.

The internment story and Ms. Ito's novel speak not just to me and my grandmother, but also our entire country. Whether one is Asian American, American Indian, Protestant, Jewish, gay or anyone considered a minority, exile is in all of our histories. The same Seattle jail cells used for those Japanese leaders in 1941 are being used today for Muslim and Arab Americans. Both detained without formal charges or legal aid in many cases. The lessons from this novel are still pertinent to our lives today.

Ms. Ito gives us the knowledge of her experience and that of countless others. Her novel is her effort to reach out and share a part of her soul. What will each of us do with her gift? How can we pass on that knowledge to someone else? Just like the Army volunteers or draft resisters, each of us has our own path and can make a difference for the good of us all.

Emily Hanako Momohara is a photographer, instructor, and graduate student at the University of Kansas, Lawrence. She holds a BFA in photography and a BA in art history from the University of Washington. She is currently serving as president of Friends of Minidoka, a nonprofit organization dedicated to preserving the history of Japanese American internment, internment civil liberties issues and diversity appreciation.

## Preface

When my granddaughter, Nicole Shinoda, was little, she would ask a lot of questions, as most youngsters do. Whenever she wanted to know about anything or anyone, she would pester whoever was within hearing distance with a string of questions that left them grasping for answers. Then she would top them off with a string of "Why's?" Today she is a senior in high school and is still asking questions with the same intensity. It was her insistence on learning about my experiences in Minidoka Relocation Center in Idaho during World War II that led me to write this book. She wanted to know why the U.S. government forced 120,000 Japanese and Japanese Americans into 10 concentration camps scattered across the western states and how I survived it. I realized it was important for her to know the truth through my eyes.

I had difficulty starting the book because of all the past negative feelings and anger that welled up within me, and days went by without a word being written. In desperation, I signed up for "Introduction to Fiction Writing" at California State University at Fullerton, and talked to instructor Patricia McFall about my writer's block. She suggested I write in the third person, and that is how the character Tomi emerged. With Patricia's guidance and encouragement, the book began to take shape. Although it is written as a work of fiction, it is based on true incidents that I observed and researched and what my family went through during the incarceration at Puyallup and Minidoka.

Another round of writer's block stalled my work and lasted three years. It was only through the gentle prodding of Doris Fritz, who had been editing the manuscript, that I finally finished the book. More important, Doris, a close friend and confidant, never lost her faith in me and waited patiently for the unproductive phase to pass. It is with gratitude and pride that I acknowledge her role in helping me finish this book before my 80th birthday.

It is my intention to convey to my granddaughter how fragile freedom really is and that it is not to be taken lightly and thrown around casually as a "constitutional right." She should know that what happened in 1942 was the result of another era in our government's history, one marked by racial discrimination, political travesty and war hysteria. To its credit, the government has since admitted the injustice of Executive Order 9066. On August 10, 1988, President Ronald Reagan signed the redress bill, HR 442. Then in 1990 an apology by President George Bush accompanied a redress payment of $20,000 each to approximately 62,500 survivors of the concentration camps. This was accomplished through the herculean efforts of determined and dedicated *nisei* and *sansei* groups that started in Seattle in 1970 and gradually spread to form a national alliance supporting the redress movement.

It is my fervent hope that Nicole and others in her generation will continue to be involved in grass-root politics and social concerns, not only for themselves but also for the whole nation. It is only through the vigilance of the next generation will the Constitution of the United States remain intact without adulteration. Their future is clearly at stake.

TOSHIKO SHOJI ITO
JUNE 2005

# 1

## Pearl Harbor

The damp morning air seeped through a crescent-shaped crack in the bedroom window, and the slapping of the shade against the windowpane drew Tomi's attention to the beginning of another dreary winter's day in Seattle. She groped for her eyeglasses and focused on the clock, which showed it was 7 a.m., and her eyes turned to the large calendar next to the dresser. It was Sunday, December 7, 1941.

Tomi's small face was framed by thick, black hair, which she wore at shoulder length and neatly clipped into a side part with a long bobby pin. Her unmade face was almost plain but had a quality of naive innocence that forgave her lack of beauty. Her dark brown eyes were hidden behind a pair of large, gold-rimmed glasses that made her face appear even smaller. She was 17 but her body lacked maturity, and she was always mistaken for someone much younger.

Miss Nellie Parker, the church youth advisor, had called the night before to ask Tomi to substitute for the regular pianist at the Japanese Presbyterian Church. Miss Parker was a leggy spinster whose hawk-like nose and narrow face reminded Tomi of a wicked witch instead of a kindly, young youth leader. She always spoke very softly in a hesitant voice that ended with a quick smile. She liked to refer to Tomi and her rambunctious girlfriends as "the handmaidens of God," bringing silent snickers from the girls.

Tomi planned to go to church early on this day to practice the hymns. She ran down the steep flight of stairs to the kitchen where her mother, Kiku, was preparing to leave for work as a housemaid for Mrs. Isaac, who lived in a beautiful, spacious house up in the hills of Seattle. Mrs. Isaac had pleaded with Kiku to come to work that Sunday and promised to pay her extra. She had a special luncheon on Monday and needed Kiku to help set it up. As soon as Kiku saw her daughter, she let loose a barrage of instructions as she put on her coat and hat.

"Be sure you do a load of wash after you get home from church. Make sure you stack some wood in the living room and practice your piano. And don't forget to pick up some bread and milk at Shimbo's!" Kiku spoke hurriedly in Japanese with occasional broken English mixed in.

"Yeah," Tomi responded in a low, sulky tone.

"*Nani?*" her mother responded. "What? Is that a proper way to speak to me?"

Tomi corrected herself, "Yes, Mama."

Kiku flung a disapproving glance at her daughter as she hurried out the kitchen door. She was shorter and heavier than her daughter, and like most Japanese women in their 50s, she hid her figure in loose-fitting, matronly clothes, covered with a full-length apron. Her right eye had a slight droop, which made her look as if she were angry, and her white hair added years to her age.

Tomi glanced out the window and watched her mother's small figure hurrying down the alley to catch the bus. She wished her mother wouldn't always be so edgy and cranky. She poked her head into the small pantry where the icebox stood. The smell of stale ice penetrated Tomi's nostrils as she opened the icebox and reached up to pull on the short, metal cord that was attached to a small, dingy light bulb. She spotted an orange in the back of the icebox and pulled out a bottle of milk for her cereal.

She finished her breakfast and rushed out the back door, banging the screen behind her. She walked up the hill to meet her friend, Mabel, who always walked to church with her.

Mabel was a few inches taller than Tomi, and chubby. Her dark brown hair was parted in the middle and tightly curled to her scalp, and her yellowish face was covered with pockmarks. She had small eyes that seemed to disappear when she smiled. Mabel's mother explained many times that Mabel had contracted typhoid fever when she was a baby and the illness left her with kinky hair and pockmarks on her skin. It seemed she wanted to make sure that everyone knew Mabel was not born that way. In spite of her looks, Mabel always managed to be cheerful and upbeat. Together they walked toward the church, which was about two miles from the house. They took a shortcut that criss-crossed down a long, steep, unpaved hill with a dirt path worn down by people trampling the same trail year after year.

Tomi decided to confide in Mabel about her dislike of attending high school.

"You know, as far as I'm concerned the only reason I go to Parkland High is because of Miss Sidney, our home room teacher. She's so different."

"How?" asked Mabel absently.

"Well, you know how Miss Sidney likes to talk about people and stuff. It's interesting." Tomi's thoughts drifted to Miss Sidney and the half-smile she always had on her face behind her gold-rimmed glasses. She would stand in front of the room, stylishly dressed and coiffured, with her hands folded in front of her. She would spew inordinate statements like, "A woman can do anything a man can. In fact, *anyone* can be anything they want to be."

But Tomi knew immediately she had made a mistake in taking Mabel into her confidence. How would a girl who always made A's in school understand? She let the conversation drop, and they trudged down the dirt path in silence until they got to the bottom of the hill, which opened onto Jackson Street and to the church.

Tomi was glad she didn't share with Mabel how she secretly admired the bold stance that Miss Sidney often took. After all, most Japanese students thought her views were radical. More importantly, when Tomi escaped into her fantasy world, Miss Sidney never humiliated or degraded her in front of the class as the other teachers did. She seemed to understand and respect Tomi's need to withdraw.

She would say lightly, "Tomi, eyes front, please." And then Tomi's walls would crumble, easing her back into reality. Mabel would never understand that part of Tomi's world.

The Japanese Presbyterian Church was brimming with people. Small children dressed in their Sunday best squealed and played tag while their parents frantically chased them. Reverend Nakamura whisked past the girls with a cheery greeting and hurried into the sanctuary. Tomi and Mabel moved to the adjoining room where the youth group was meeting and peered in to see if any boys were there. They were disappointed to see only Tad and his brother Mark fighting in the back. The boys were much too young for the girls, and Tomi and Mabel wrinkled their noses and giggled. They spotted a few of their friends at the front of the room and joined them. Miss Parker started the worship service with her nervous smile and asked Tomi to start the opening hymn, "Sweet Hour of Prayer."

On the way home from church, Tomi and Mabel stopped by the Pioneer Bakery and were surprised to find it open on Sunday. The bakery was a long building with high square windows and a small storefront. The girls could see the freshly wrapped bread and pastries sitting in the showcase through the sparkling clean windows, and the enticing aroma of freshly baked bread drew them inside. Tomi and Mabel went directly to the counter and each picked a package of chocolate Hostess cupcakes.

"That will be 5 cents today," said Mrs. Robins, peering through the stack of bread on the high counter. "You know, I'm usually not open in the front on Sunday. You caught me at the right time."

"I only have 4 cents. Can you lend me a penny, Tomi?"

"How come you're always broke? Tomi complained. This is the second time this week!"

Mabel pouted, making her pudgy face look even rounder.

"Oh okay, here's your penny," sighed Tomi.

"By the way, girls," said Mrs. Robins, "I thought I heard something about a bombing in Hawaii. Have you heard anything? I haven't had time to sit down and really listen to the radio."

"No, we haven't heard anything," said Tomi. "Besides, the war is in Europe, Mrs. Robins."

"Well, guess I better go check the news anyway," said Mrs. Robins as she turned away.

Tomi unwrapped one cupcake and stuffed the other into her sweater pocket. She savored the taste of the fresh, moist cupcake and allowed the rich flavor to linger in her mouth. She looked over at Mabel and saw her face covered with chocolate crumbs and frosting; some of the crumbs had rolled into the cavities of her scars.

"Boy, you look funny!" said Tomi. "You got chocolate all over yourself."

They both roared with laughter. The girls finished their cupcakes and sauntered toward home with their arms locked together.

"Hey, I wonder what Mrs. Robins was talking about?" said Mabel. "All that stuff about bombing and Hawaii."

"Guess she heard one of those radio dramas, huh?" laughed Tomi.

"You think there's anything to it?" asked Mabel.

"Nah."

They finally parted company at the bottom of the hill where Tomi lived.

"Don't forget you owe me 3 cents," Tomi said over her shoulder and heard Mabel giggle.

Tomi looked up the hill at her house. The house was facing the street that was lined with tall maple trees. There was an alley running parallel to the house that led to the next block. She could see the large, empty lot full of overgrown bushes and weeds that crept up to the alley. Because the house was built with a basement, the weakened foundation was starting to cause it to tilt. Every time Tomi baked a cake in the small gas oven, the cake would come out slanted. She would stack the cakes in the opposite direction to compensate for the slant and fill in the dips with frosting.

As Tomi glanced up she caught a speck of light in the kitchen window. She walked up the hill and entered through the back door. George, her older brother, was sitting at the kitchen table, and she vaguely wondered why he was home. Ever since he started at the University of Washington, he was never around, especially on Sundays. George was a handsome young man with jet-black hair that ended in a mass of ringlets on his forehead. He had fine features, and his long, lean figure had yet to peak into manhood.

"How come you're home, George?" she asked as she walked to the small potbelly stove in the corner of the room.

George didn't answer her.

She held her hands over the stove to warm herself and glanced casually at her brother, who was listening intently to the radio.

"Didn't you hear me," she started to say, but George's voice cut in sharply. "Listen!"

Tomi edged closer to the radio and heard the staccato voice of the announcer blare out, "Japan has bombed Pearl Harbor!"

"What? That can't be true! Mrs. Robins was right."

George wasn't listening to her. He was glued to the radio. He turned the volume up as if to drown out Tomi's outburst. His face was etched in a tight expression, and he drew his arms together into a tight knot across his chest.

"Oh my God," he gasped. "It's true! We're probably going to war with Japan."

The voice on the radio droned on about the treachery of Japan and proceeded to fill in the details of the bombing. Tomi was stunned by the news and hardly heard the announcer's voice crescendo into a high pitch as he continued to describe the bombing of the U.S. military bases and the countless dead and wounded.

She looked at her brother and asked, "What's going to happen to us, George? What are we going to do?"

George answered quickly. "What are you worried about? We're Americans. Nothing is going to happen—that's a dumb question! Ha…," his voice trailed off. His bravado wasn't convincing. Both of them were well aware of their low status as Japanese Americans in the white community of Seattle. Instinctively, they knew that the bombing of Pearl Harbor would be laid at their feet, and the reality struck home with unspoken fear and worry. Tomi's thoughts turned to her mother, and she wished Kiku was home with them.

"I'd better call Mama at Mrs. Isaac's," Tomi said tersely.

"Okay, call," said George. "What about Papa?"

"He should be home from the market soon—it's almost 2 o'clock. He'll be okay." Tomi wasn't worried about her father. He was invincible. Saburo Inouye ruled his home with an iron hand. His word was law, and his commands went unchallenged. Nothing could harm him, she thought.

The phone rang. It was Mack Hara, Tomi's boyfriend. His usually calm voice was tense.

"Guess you heard the news about the bombing, huh? Are you guys okay?" he asked. "There are all kinds of wild rumors flying around that the FBI is on a rampage and picking people up. Not only that, but I hear they'll be rounding up everybody who is of Japanese descent and putting them in internment camps."

"Don't be silly, Mack. How can they put us in camps? We're Americans! They can't throw us into camps! They wouldn't do that to us."

"I just don't know. I can't think right now. My mother is in hysterics, but don't tell your mother. You know how the *issei* [first generation] are about those things. By the way, there's a JACL emergency meeting tonight at the Nippon Kan. I think we'd better go."

"Okay, Mack, pick me up around 6:30. Look, I've got to call my mother at work and make sure she's okay," Tomi said hurriedly and hung up.

She turned to George as she dialed Mrs. Isaac's number and told him about the JACL meeting.

"Did you know there are rumors already about rounding up the Japanese Americans?"

"Ah…bunch of rumors, that's all! The JACL will know what the score is. They'll know what to do. I'll go to the meeting with you guys tonight."

The Japanese-American Citizens League to which they both belonged was a young, national organization that bridged the gap between the young and older generations and encouraged the assimilation of the young *nisei* (second generation, American-born Japanese). Tomi was confident that the JACL leaders would have the answers to all these wild rumors, but now she was getting uneasy. She felt the force of panic hit her stomach and fought to keep it from overwhelming her. She knew better than to give in to her feelings—she had been taught to be in control of them at all times. It was a sign of weakness to show fear or any other emotion.

The radio was still blaring out details of the devastation off the shores of the Hawaiian islands—the sinking American battleships, the twisted wreckage of the American planes on the airfield, and the unknown plight of the American soldiers.

"George, turn that darn radio off. I can't think!" she yelled.

George glared at her as he hovered over the radio but turned the volume down and continued to devour the news.

Kiku was still at Mrs. Isaac's home when the news of Pearl Harbor was announced. The two women were preparing for the big luncheon and the kitchen was bustling with activity. Mrs. Isaac's best silverware and china were being polished and cleaned. Buckets of fresh flowers from the local flower shop sat on the back porch.

Mrs. Isaac heard the news of the bombing on the radio as she was polishing her silverware. Her hands froze in midair as the grim news was announced.

"Kiku!" she screamed. "Come here quickly!"

Kiku responded to the urgency of Mrs. Isaac's voice and ran into the kitchen.

"What, Mrs. Isaac? What's wrong?"

"Japan has bombed Pearl Harbor, Kiku!" The two women looked at each other and said nothing. Kiku searched Mrs. Isaac's face for signs of reassurance, but none was forthcoming. The phone rang, and it was Tomi asking about her mother. Mrs. Isaac assured her that Kiku would be on her way home soon.

"I go now," said Kiku in her broken English and turned to leave. Like most *issei*, Kiku was aware of the tension that had existed between the United States and Japan for many years, but she never thought a war would break out between the two nations.

Mrs. Isaac's voice was almost whiny. "Please, Kiku. This war does not concern you and me. I need you tomorrow. You must come back to help me. I have 20 women coming for lunch tomorrow. You can't leave me alone with all this work! What am I going to do?"

Kiku was incredulous. The world was at war, and all this woman could think about was her luncheon. Isn't that like a *hakujin*, she thought angrily. "I try," she said as she gathered her belongings and hurried out the back door with Mrs. Isaac's pleading voice following her.

"Call me if you can't make it...."

Kiku rushed to the bus stop and felt uneasy. What if the people on the bus singled her out? What could she do? She started to feel frightened.

The commuters started to gather as Kiku waited anxiously. The bus finally arrived, and she was swept into the packed vehicle where strangers were exchanging comments in loud, tense voices about Pearl Harbor and "those dirty Japs." She tried to be inconspicuous, and no one paid any attention to her. Relieved, Kiku got off at her stop and hurried up the hill to the safety of her home.

# 2

## Burning the Past

Tomi's fears were beginning to escalate. The more she listened to the radio, the more anxious she got. Now they were talking about declaring war on Japan officially, and she worried about how her *hakujin* friends at the high school would treat her. She dreaded the thought of facing them tomorrow. She felt the knot in her stomach tighten and leaned back hard in her chair to control it.

George glanced at Tomi and wondered if she was aware of how seriously the ramifications of the bombing would affect them. She was such a baby at times. He was sure he would be drafted if war broke out with Japan and was annoyed at the thought of having to give up his education. He would have been the first one in the family to be a university graduate, and now it would probably have to be put on the back burner. He vaguely wondered how his father would react to the news about Japan bombing Pearl Harbor. There was no way to tell with his father's dark mood.

\* \* \*

Saburo arrived home shortly after his wife, and his usual surly demeanor was subdued. He entered through the front door and walked into the kitchen without a word. Saburo was almost 20 years older than his wife but looked considerably younger than his 69 years. He had thick, gray hair and wore horn-rimmed glasses. He was slender but muscular and stood about 4 inches shorter than his son. Saburo's presence always created a tense atmosphere at home because of his volatile temper, which erupted frequently without provocation. Today his usual swagger was missing. He was visibly shaken.

"What a catastrophe this is!" Saburo said in Japanese. "Why would Japan do a thing like this? I do not understand what is going on. Mr. Goto gave me a ride home today because he thought there might be trouble for me on the bus. Anyway, I helped him close the market, but he plans on opening up tomorrow morning." Saburo sat down at the table in the small kitchen as Kiku served him tea.

"Are you going in to work tomorrow?" asked Kiku.

"I have to. There is a delivery of chickens coming in tomorrow and Mr. Goto needs someone to prepare them for the market. If I do not go, I will not get paid."

Usually, when Saburo walked into the room, Tomi and George would vanish quietly to their own rooms and leave Kiku to deal with his outbursts. Kiku usually had no escape from his lashing tongue. It took the news of Pearl Harbor to pull the family together. Kiku took the opportunity to talk lightly about Mrs. Isaac's luncheon tomorrow, and they laughed ruefully at her shallowness. George turned up the radio again and tried to explain to his parents what the announcers were saying about the attack. He was having a difficult time translating the intricate terminology concerning the war and spoke in a halting manner in English and broken Japanese. Like most *nisei*, George and Tomi had attended Japanese language school after their regular school hours but never mastered the language to a high degree of fluency.

The phone rang insistently. Kiku answered.

"Yes, Hiro, my husband is home. You wish to come over and speak with him? One moment, please."

Kiku turned to Saburo and said, "It's young Hiro Wada—you know, Mr. Wada's oldest son. He's on the phone and wishes to come over and talk to you about something very important."

Saburo closed his eyes, reached under his glasses and pressed his fingers between his eyes as he lowered his head.

"Tell him I am busy."

"He insists."

"Very well, tell him to come over," Saburo said in a low voice.

Tomi thought it was strange that Hiro wanted to make such an untimely visit. The Wadas lived a couple of blocks away in a huge house, and she never liked Hiro. As a child, he had a reputation for being the neighborhood bully. His short, burly body matched the ugly scowl on his face. Tomi exchanged quick glances with her brother at their father's reaction. George shrugged his shoulders and raised his eyebrows.

The family moved into the living room to wait for Hiro, as Kiku prepared tea for the guest. Saburo sank into his favorite leather chair while Tomi and George sat around the wooden table that took up most of the living room. A large potbelly stove with cast iron legs was squeezed into the corner and the warmth it generated quickly filled the small room. An uneasy silence settled over the family as they retreated into their own thoughts.

Saburo drummed his fingers on the arms of his chair. He knew what Hiro Wada wanted. Hiro's father had stopped by the market to ask him to pay back the money that Saburo borrowed years ago to open a market on Pike Street.

"I am sorry to ask you to pay me part of the loan, but now that war with Japan is imminent, I may need the money for my family," Mr. Wada said to Saburo earlier in the day.

How was he to know that the Great Depression would wipe him out, thought Saburo. All he had now was his low-paying job at Mr. Goto's market. He hated being obligated to Wada-san and should have never asked for the loan. Now he had to deal with Wada-san's son and be humiliated in front of his own family. His thoughts faded as he heard George speak to him.

"Papa, did you know the FBI is thinking of rounding up the community leaders?" asked George. "Have you heard anything?"

"All I know is Mr. Goto advised me to burn anything that might be pro-Japanese and get rid of any incriminating documents. This is one time being poor will pay off for me," Saburo said wryly. "I have nothing of value. Let them come and take me—I have nothing to hide." He slumped back in his chair and slowly ran his fingers through his hair. "By the way, George, I want you to take that picture of the emperor that's hanging in the living room and burn it. Right now."

"That's ridiculous. It's only a picture!" exclaimed George.

"I said *now!*"

"Papa, that's not what the FBI will be looking for."

"How dare you talk back to me! I gave you an order! Do it now!" Saburo's voice rose to a high pitch, and he clutched the arms of the chair as if to jump up. Just as George wheeled around to confront his father, a loud, persistent knock was heard at the front door. Both men immediately relaxed their stance but continued to glare at each other.

Tomi started to open the front door for Hiro Wada, who angrily pushed his way in and demanded, "Where's your father? I want to see him right now!" Without waiting for an answer he brushed rudely past her and barged into the living room. Hiro stood in front of Saburo with arms akimbo. His face was full of contempt as he bellowed, "Mr. Inouye, you know why I am here. My father told me he went down to the market today, and you refused to pay the money you owe him. What kind of crap is that?" The words sputtered from his mouth as he spoke.

"Ooh," gasped Tomi. She was horrified at Hiro's rudeness to

his elder.

George's head snapped back as he muttered, "What the heck…?" He scraped his chair back to lunge at Hiro.

Hearing the commotion, Kiku rushed into the living room in time to step in front of George and stop him. She had never heard such disrespect coming from someone outside her family, especially from someone as young as Hiro, and she was bewildered by his behavior.

"What is it? What is the meaning of this disturbance?"

George side-stepped his mother and placed himself between Hiro and his father. "Where do you get off coming in here and yelling like that! Get out of here!"

Ignoring George, Saburo spoke quietly. He looked past Hiro as if in a trance, his face pale and drawn.

"This matter is between your father and me. I don't wish to discuss it with you. It's none of your business."

"Don't treat me like a child. This *is* my business. Don't forget I am the oldest son of the Wada family. I have the right to be here."

With flailing arms, Hiro continued his tirade as Saburo sat watching him, allowing him to vent his anger. Finally, Saburo could no longer retain his composure. He leaped out of his chair and thundered at Hiro, "Silence! I will not have you speak to me in that tone of voice in my own house. You will leave NOW!"

Hiro was taken aback by Saburo's bold stance and he reeled back a couple of steps. Hiro was not aware of Saburo's violent temper, which he rarely displayed in public. He was not expecting this quiet-mannered man who never voiced his opinion in public to show any resistance. Hiro thought his prey would be easily subdued. His voice faltered as he backed away from Saburo and made his way toward the front door. "You—you know you're wrong, Mr. Inouye. No matter what, you still owe my father a lot of money!" The front door slammed shut with a resounding crash as Hiro stomped out of the house.

The awkward silence in the room was deafening. Tomi could actually hear the ringing in her ears grow louder. Not wanting to witness her father's humiliation any further, she looked away from him. Kiku busied herself with the tray and teacups and quietly moved into the kitchen. George sat slumped in his chair and pushed his hands deep into his pockets as Saburo stood alone by his chair with clenched fists. Saburo turned to his son and said, "Now, I want you to get that picture and burn it."

George slowly got up from his chair and left the room without a word. As much as he hated his father's tyranny, he could not allow him to be stripped of all his dignity and pride. In a few moments he returned with the picture of the emperor and threw it into the potbelly stove. He watched the flames swirl around the picture and turn it into ashes. As he closed the heavy iron door, he could see the twisted outline of the wires that held the frame as it glowed brightly.

# 3

# The Town Hall Meeting

Bill Imada was about to break the law. His heart beat rapidly, and he tried to control his shaking hands as he picked up his briefcase. Bill was slightly stocky and in his late 20s. His round face had a wide mouth that frequently broke into a pleasant smile and put people at ease, but tonight he was not smiling. As he sat in his old, rickety Chevrolet sedan, he watched the orderly crowd file into the Nippon Kan, the local theater and meeting place for the Japanese community. Bill knew he was about to commit a crime in the eyes of the government, but as a young, budding lawyer he could not stand by and watch his peers and their parents be incarcerated by the U.S. government. Perhaps this initial meeting with the JACL would give him the opportunity to talk about the Bill of Rights and help the community understand that what the government intended to do was unconstitutional. What was more troubling was the acquiescence of the Japanese community as a whole.

Bill was fully aware that his quest for justice was not a popular one. As a matter of fact, he had already been warned by the Japanese community leaders not to create trouble. They explained to him that they trusted the government and had faith that the right thing would be done. He had searched his conscience for hours and pored over the law books and, in the end, made a decision to take a stand. Tonight he would try to get his message across that if the government decided to incarcerate those of Japanese descent, they must be ready to resist. Bill knew he was in for a hard fight. He had the dubious task of convincing the victims of their impending doom, and he was not looking forward to it.

Mack, Tomi's boyfriend, parked his car near the building. He was a handsome young man in his early 20s who had an affinity for natty clothes. His chiseled good looks matched his lanky stride. His eyelids brushed the top of his eyes, giving him a slumberous look. Tomi admired his taste in clothes but was more impressed that he was one of the few *nisei* who owned a car, a spanking new Ford at that. She got out of the car, looked around and spotted Bill walking toward the entrance.

"Isn't that Bill Imada?" she asked.

"Yeah, you're right, Tomi, it is," Mack said and hailed Bill as he walked by. "Hi, Bill. What's going on tonight?"

Bill acknowledged everyone in his usual pleasant manner and said, "Well, you probably heard by now that I'm not happy with the way the JACL is telling the community to cooperate if the government decides to relocate us. I'm going to try to persuade these people to rethink this whole situation and let them know that the government's action would be unconstitutional and that we should fight it."

Mack cocked his head and answered, "You know, Bill, you're asking for trouble. You can't fight the government. They can do whatever they want. How are we going to fight the whole damn system? The *hakujins* hate us as it is."

"I know, I know. But if we fight this and go to court, we might be able to win," said Bill.

"You're crazy," chimed in George. "We'd probably be shot like dogs if we did that. Look, Bill, every time something happens we get blamed for it. As long as we work hard as cheap labor and keep our mouths shut, the *hakujins* are happy. As soon as we get ambitious and start getting successful, they pass all kinds of laws to prevent us from succeeding."

"Yeah, and now I hear they're already blaming us for spying for the Japanese government," said Tomi. "Can you imagine?"

"I was hoping I could count on you, Mack," Bill said.

Mack looked uncomfortable and did not reply. Like most *nisei* he was not willing to create any commotion and resented Bill for putting him on the spot.

Mack finally mumbled, "Guess not."

Excusing himself, Bill walked away quickly and entered the building.

The Nippon Kan hall was filled to capacity. The clattering of wooden chairs echoed in the hall as the young men scurried to set them up. The wooden floors squeaked as the people shuffled in and took their seats. There was a huge, bright reddish-yellow curtain that stretched across the stage. On the curtain were large squares that were rented out to the local merchants for advertisements. There was only one empty space.

The crowd consisted mostly of young *nisei* and leaders of the community. Tomi noticed the absence of Mr. Matsumoto and Mr. Arai, who were the most influential *issei* leaders in the community. She spotted Bill Imada at the edge of the stage speaking to the JACL leaders as they huddled together. Tomi moved toward the group to invite Bill to sit with Mack and George. Before she could reach him, a commotion erupted between Bill and the JACL leaders.

Suddenly all eyes in the auditorium turned to the members of the group as their voices started to rise. Their heads jerked and jabbing fingers emphasized each angry word. One of the *issei* leaders quickly herded them all behind the curtain, where they resumed their argument. Tomi hurried behind the curtain to find Bill Imada fuming. He had been removed from the agenda as one of the main speakers and was demanding an explanation from Jack Mori, the president of the local JACL.

"This is not the time to play politics!" he yelled at Jack. "I insist on being put back on the agenda."

"Keep your voice down, Bill. What are you trying to do? Start a riot? Those people sitting out there don't know Matsumoto and Arai were just picked up by the FBI. If you get them stirred up now, for whatever reason, we're going to have one hell of a mess. I'm taking you off the agenda. I can't risk you causing any trouble. I'll handle it," said Jack. He was well aware of Bill's radical views and intentions. Jack had just started his junior year at the University of Washington and was majoring in business administration. He was an idealistic, energetic young man who took his role seriously as JACL president.

"Maybe I can't do anything about Matsumoto and Arai right now, but all I want to do is to let everyone know that the government can't impose a relocation order without violating our civil rights. Why can't you see that?" Bill was beginning to look disheveled and agitated.

Tosh Mukai was an insurance salesman who was older than the other two men. He put his hands on Bill's shoulder condescendingly. "Don't you think our job is to keep everyone calm? Let's stick with the issue at hand. We really don't know if we are going to be relocated yet. Besides, since when did civil rights laws ever apply to us? There's no sense jumping the gun."

An exasperated Bill answered, "That's the whole point! We *are* covered by civil rights in this country. But by the time we get organized, it'll be too late. Time is of the essence."

The young men continued their heated argument with neither side conceding. Finally, Jack cut Bill off. "It's final! That's it. You're not on the agenda tonight. Now, if you want to stay, okay, but not as a speaker!"

Jack turned on his heel abruptly and walked onto the stage with Tosh close behind him. Dejected, Bill picked up his briefcase and slowly walked down a short wooden staircase leading back into the auditorium as curious eyes followed him. Tomi went back to her seat without speaking to Bill. It didn't seem the appropriate time to speak to him after the confrontation. She whispered to Mack and George what she had just overheard, and both men shook their heads in disbelief.

The meeting began with Mr. Shotaro Konno announcing in Japanese the shocking news of Zentaro Matsumoto and Kanji Arai's arrest by the FBI when they arrived for the meeting. The crowd responded with noisy disbelief and shock. Mr. Konno, who was one of the *issei* leaders, pleaded with the crowd to remain calm. He spoke for several minutes on maintaining the dignity and pride of the Japanese community. Although the evening was damp and cold, Mr. Konno's bald forehead was beaded with perspiration, and he kept dabbing it with a large white handkerchief. Most of the *nisei* did not understand Mr. Konno's elaborate Japanese phrases, but his passionate plea and emotions were clearly conveyed.

After acknowledging Mr. Konno, Jack took over the meeting and expressed his regret concerning the arrest of the two *issei* leaders. He appealed to the audience to keep a level head and echoed Mr. Konno's message.

"Let us not lose sight of the fact that we do not have the facts concerning the arrest of Mr. Matsumoto and Mr. Arai," Jack said. "I'm sure you are aware that the U.S. government will not hold them for no reason at all. As soon as they are checked out, I am sure their release will be imminent. Let us have faith in our own country and its justice system. As a matter of fact, allow me to read you this wire, which was sent to President Roosevelt by the National JACL as soon as the news of Pearl Harbor was announced today:

*In this solemn hour we pledge our fullest cooperation to*

*you, Mr. President, and to our country. There cannot be any question. There must be no doubt. We in our hearts know we are Americans loyal to America. We must prove that to all of you.*

This solemn proclamation was met with a low murmur of approval from the crowd and escalated into resounding applause.

Jack proceeded to talk about the *nisei's* responsibility to look after their parents and other *issei* who might need help. "Make sure they know what is transpiring," he said. He went on to remind them of the repercussions that would probably follow the declaration of war with Japan that was expected to be announced tomorrow by the United States. He emphasized the importance of keeping a cool head against those who may try to provoke a fight or hurl racial insults at them.

He concluded his speech by repeating, "We must do all we can to prove that we are loyal Americans, and we must cooperate with the government of the United States in every way possible."

Tomi leaned over to George and said, "Now, that makes a lot of sense."

"I'm not too sure about anything. I just hope Jack knows what he's doing." George frowned. "I just can't put my fingers on it, but something is wrong."

"You're such a worrywart, George!"

"Oh, shut up! What do you know?"

As the meeting broke up, the crowd filed out in a pensive mood. Tomi walked down the steps with Mack and George, and she saw her friend Mabel standing with her mother, Yae Kane. They had arrived late to the meeting and rushed over to Tomi.

"Have you heard the latest?" said Mabel breathlessly. "Reverend Hata of the Buddhist Church was picked up by the FBI an hour ago."

"For what?" asked Tomi.

"Do they have to have a reason?" Yae said bitterly, more of a statement than a question.

The people moved slowly past them, and the news of Reverend Hata's arrest filtered quickly through the crowd, adding to its distress.

Mack was bothered by his conversation with Bill Imada before the meeting. He respected Bill and didn't want to leave with any misunderstanding. He was even more concerned after what Tomi had witnessed just before the start of the meeting. Giving his key to George, he asked him to wait in the car with Tomi and caught Bill just as he was getting into his sedan.

"Bill, I have to talk to you. It's important," he said, but Bill was not in the mood to talk. His mind was whirling with frustration. He knew why certain *issei* were picked up and was not anxious to share that information with anyone yet. He just learned of Reverend Hata's arrest. No, Bill couldn't deal with Mack or anyone else tonight.

Mack rested his foot on the running board and said, "Bill, I don't know what went on between you and Jack before the meeting, but I'm sorry you didn't get to speak tonight. It's not that I don't support you, but I'm really confused about the whole damn thing. I want to hear your side of the argument."

Bill sucked in his breath and let it out slowly. "Okay, but you know, Mack, I'm not good for anything right now. I'm really shot. Why don't we meet tomorrow at Joe's Cafe around 6 o'clock? You might as well bring Tomi and her brother, George. I have something to tell you and they need to hear it too." Mack and Bill solemnly shook hands and went their separate ways.

The ride home from the meeting was unusually quiet. The events of the day had been taxing, and Mack was worried about his mother. She had not taken the news of the Pearl Harbor bombing well. It was not like her to go into hysterics, and his father was still trying to calm her down when Mack left for the meeting. He also wondered if the FBI would target his father because of his involvement with the Japanese Community Center. So far, only the community leaders had been picked up by the FBI. He wondered what information Bill had that was so confidential. But right now, he just wanted to get home.

Tomi was exhausted. All the events leading up to the meeting had been building tension all day, and now Mabel's news about Reverend Hata's arrest was the last straw. Everyone knew Reverend Hata was dedicated to the welfare of the Japanese community and counted on him in times of crisis. Why would they pick up a fine person like him? She suddenly remembered that she would have to face her Caucasian friends at school tomorrow. She felt the knot in her stomach tighten even more.

George was also worried. Within the last two hours, three top community leaders had been arrested, all of them *issei*. More arrests were probably pending. He had to agree with his father, Saburo, that being poor and uninvolved would probably be their salvation from arrest. He thought about his conversation with Bill and wondered whether there really was the possibility of fighting the relocation order if the government imposed it. Mack's voice cut through his thoughts.

"Bill wants to meet with all of us tomorrow night at 6 o'clock at Joe's Cafe. He says he has something important to tell us."

They rode in silence for the rest of the way home. Mack let Tomi and George off in front of their house and promised to come back around 5:30 p.m. the following day. The Ford made a noisy exit down the cobblestone hill and the fading sound of backfire could be heard as he drove away.

\* \* \*

As soon as Mack walked up to the unlit porch of his house, he sensed something was wrong. There was a dim light in the back of the kitchen, and his dog, Jackie, lay whimpering by the front door, which was partially open. He could feel his heart pounding as he pushed it all the way and noticed that the damp December air had crept into the living room.

"Mama! Papa!"

There was no answer. Mack groped for the light switch and looked around wildly. The room was littered with paper, and books had been pulled out and thrown on the floor. Drawers from his father's desk had been pulled out and the contents strewn everywhere. Mack knew then that the FBI had been there.

He called again, "Mama! Where are you?"

He saw that the door to his parents' bedroom was closed and flung it open. The room was in total disarray. The mattress had been pulled away from the bed and flung on the floor. All the bureau drawers had been rummaged through and dumped out. He heard a faint sob from the other side of the bed and found his mother on the floor. She was kneeling with her face buried in her hands. Her body was shaking with quiet sobs as she rocked back and forth.

"Oh, my God," Mack whispered.

He wanted to hold and comfort her, but his upbringing compelled him to keep his emotions in check. He knelt down beside her and awkwardly touched her shoulder. He had never seen his mother break down and found it painful to watch.

They remained in repose with neither one able to speak. Gradually, her sobbing subsided and her body began to relax. Hanako Hara wiped her eyes with her apron. She was ashamed to have her son find her in such an emotional state. It was bad enough that she became hysterical over the news of Pearl Harbor this afternoon, but when the FBI barged into the house a couple of hours ago and treated her husband, Masaaki, with such disrespect and disdain, she could not contain herself. The two agents had ransacked the whole house. In her eyes, their total disregard for any human decency in search of "evidence of conspiracy" was despicable. They had left abruptly with Masaaki in tow, and she was alone amid complete chaos with trails of letters and papers everywhere. She should not have allowed her son to see his mother giving in to the rage and humiliation that she felt.

As she struggled to get up, Mack gently helped her. He searched her face to offer solace, but she would not look at him.

"What happened? Where's Papa?" Mack asked, trying to keep his own emotions in check.

Hanako turned away from her son and said, "I am so ashamed to have acted this way. Please forgive me. Your father has been arrested, and he will need our support. I do not know where they have taken him, but he is all right. We must be strong. After all, we cannot fight this. *Shikata-ga-nai.*"

She was right, Mack thought. *It couldn't be helped.*

"I am very tired. I don't want to talk about this incident anymore." As Hanako looked at her son's bewildered face, she made a vow to herself never to lose control again. She gripped her son's hand hard for a moment and let go. Slowly she walked toward the bathroom.

"Are you all right, Mama?"

"*Hai,* I am fine. You need not worry about me now."

Mack felt the anger rise in his chest. He walked back into the living room and surveyed the damage. He kicked a table lamp lying in his path and sent it shattering against the wall. "God-damned government!"

Hanako appeared at the living room door and said, "That is enough, Mack. Anger never solves anything. We will clean up tomorrow. Good night."

Still shaking with rage, Mack rummaged through the debris to pull out the telephone. He dialed and heard Bill Imada's weary voice on the other end. "Bill, this is Mack. They got my father—the FBI. They picked him up and ransacked the whole house!" Mack's voice shook with emotion as he ranted about the injustice of the raid and his frustration in not being able to do anything.

"Wait, wait," said Bill. "Calm down, Mack. I'm trying to follow what you're saying." He allowed Mack to continue venting his anger until he could no longer talk. Bill let out a loud sigh. "Mack, I don't know how to tell you this, but you should know that your father may have been turned in by the JACL. *That's* what I wanted to talk to you guys about."

"You're wrong, Bill!" Mack shouted. "Dead wrong!"

"Look. There's nothing more you or I can do tonight. Just don't discuss this with anyone until I explain what's going on with the JACL tomorrow. You'll be there at Joe's Cafe with Tomi and George, right? I'm really sorry about your father. I don't know what else to say…."

Spent with emotion, Mack answered, "Okay, Bill. You're right. Sorry I lost my head. I know you well enough to trust you. I'll see you tomorrow."

Bill hung up the receiver. For a brief moment he sat silently with his eyes closed as if to shut out the relentless series of events, which kept escalating without relief. He knew that what he had just told Mack about the JACL would split the Japanese community wide open.

# 4

## The Raid

The morning light caught the strands of thinning hair that floated across the crown of Hugh Wilson's head.

As principal of Parkland High School, he had called a special meeting on the Monday before school opened. His tall frame almost covered the podium as he leaned forward to speak to the faculty about the sensitive issues surrounding the bombing of Pearl Harbor.

Mr. Wilson was aware of the distrust and hatred directed at the Japanese community by various groups in Seattle, and he was determined to dispel any repercussions stemming from the declaration of war.

"The Japanese-American students are not to blame for what is happening between America and Japan. We must help the students to remain calm and focused. The President will address Congress this morning to officially declare war on Japan, and as educators, it is our responsibility to set an example of decorum and good faith in our students," he concluded.

* * *

Tomi was still reeling from the string of events that had taken place last night at the Nippon Kan. She deliberately timed her arrival at school this morning to avoid running into her Caucasian friends. She was not certain how they would treat her and was not willing to risk any confrontation. She could feel the knot in her stomach begin to tighten, and a dull pain throbbed in her intestines. She waited until the warning bell before walking down the long corridor to her home room.

After the faculty meeting, Tomi's home room teacher, Martha Sidney, sat at her desk watching the students file into the room. Her eyes scanned the class, and just as the tardy bell rang she saw Tomi slide into her seat.

After taking roll, she stood in front of the class and said, "This morning, our country will be at war with Japan."

The room became deathly silent as she walked slowly in the aisles between desks and continued to speak.

"It's important to remember that war is caused by philosophical and political differences between countries, and not by the people themselves. It's our duty," she continued, "to defend our country in every way possible, but it's also our duty to make sure that we do not discriminate against those who are loyal to our country."

As Miss Sidney approached Tomi's desk, her hands lightly brushed and rested on Tomi's shoulders. This startled her because she was not accustomed to any physical contact, especially one of affection. Her eyes darted to her teacher's face, which mirrored compassion, but she was flustered by the attention and did not hear the rest of Miss Sidney's speech. However, her teacher's insight calmed Tomi's fears and for the rest of day she noticed a sense of heightened awareness in each class she attended. Some of the Caucasian students who usually ignored her made it a point to go out of their way to greet her with a smile. By the time school ended, she felt as if a sense of normalcy had returned.

Tomi hurried home to find George engrossed in the *Seattle Post-Intelligencer* newspaper, which was spread out on the kitchen table. He looked up as she entered the room and without a word turned back to the paper. The siblings had never been close. As a young child, George was always sickly. As he grew older, the other boys would tease him unmercifully because he looked frail and thin for his age. The teasing led to many fistfights, which frequently drew intervention from Tomi, who was a tomboy. George deeply resented her well-intentioned meddling and often screamed at her to "Stay out of it!" Tomi would be bewildered and hurt by his reaction, but she soon learned to allow him to fight his own battles. As years passed, the chasm between the two grew wider. It was not uncommon for them to pass by without greeting each other. The only time they connected, it seemed, was in times of crisis.

"Hey, Tomi," George barked at her. "You better call Mack and tell him to meet us early at our house instead of Joe's Cafe. Oh yeah, don't forget to call Bill too. The *PI* says we may have an air raid practice tonight."

"Call them yourself," she retorted.

"Look, dummy, I just heard Mack's father was picked up last night. Don't you think you should call him?"

Tomi gasped, and her hands flew to her mouth. She looked frightened, and George was sorry he had been so blunt with her.

His voice softened as he tried to make amends. "I think Mack is waiting for you to call. We really have to meet earlier. Mack and Bill won't be able to drive their cars if we have a late air raid practice tonight, okay?"

"Okay," she said quietly as she picked up the phone and dialed Mack's number. Mack's mother answered, and Tomi addressed her politely in Japanese.

As soon as Hanako heard Tomi's voice, she hesitated for a moment before speaking. She was displeased with Tomi for calling her son. No self-respecting girl would be calling a man, she thought. Besides, this girl was too young for her son. What did he see in her anyway? "Just one moment," she said coolly and called Mack to the phone.

"Why didn't you call me about your father, Mack?" Tomi asked. "I can't believe the FBI would do such a thing!"

"Well, they did and left everything in a mess." Mack sounded almost aloof. He fell silent. Mack was feeling awkward speaking to Tomi in front of his mother, who stood nearby with her arms folded, glaring at him with pursed lips.

Tomi was at a loss for words. Mack's reluctance to elaborate prevented her from expressing her concern. Instead, she blurted out George's suggestion to meet earlier with Bill and did not wait for Mack's reply before she hung up. Tomi stood by the phone for a moment, smarting from Mack's impassive response.

"Now what's the matter?" asked George.

"Nothing," she muttered and walked away.

* * *

That evening, before Bill and Mack arrived, the air-raid siren went off. The mournful wailing echoed across the hills of Seattle and through the walls of the silent houses. It was almost dusk, and Tomi stepped off the back porch to stand in the middle of a small garden patch. Her eyes swept across the gentle rise of the hills, which were dotted with rows of houses. As the sound of the siren continued to rise and fall, she could see the tiny sparks of lights in the windows blink and fade away. Only the faint silhouette of the darkened houses remained on the hills. The dampness of the night descended, and darkness veiled the city. It was as if the whole city of Seattle had died.

When the siren finally stopped, the only sound Tomi heard was the whisper of the wind. An eerie sense of fear gripped her as she stood in the darkness, and for a moment an overwhelming feeling of helplessness swept over her and she shuddered.

Long after the lights came back on, Tomi continued to grapple with her emotions and finally accepted what she had been taught all her life. To *gaman. Endure.*

Kiku looked out the kitchen window with her arms folded across her chest and watched her young daughter struggle with her fears but made no move to comfort her. This is a journey she must make herself, she thought. I cannot walk this road for her. Life was not easy, and Tomi would have to learn to cope by herself.

As Tomi moved toward the house, Kiku opened the kitchen door to let her in and said, "Everyone is already here. Why don't you join them while I prepare some tea?" She glanced anxiously at her daughter's stoic face. Tomi walked into the living room where the men were already seated. They glanced up and casually nodded to her. She ignored Mack, who was trying to catch her eye, and took a seat between George and Bill Imada.

Bill shuffled nervously in his seat and scooted closer to the table. "I already told Mack it was possible that the JACL turned his father in."

"Why would they do that?" asked George. "What possible reason would the JACL have to turn him in?"

"Yeah," chimed in Mack. "My father isn't a Japanese spy. I would've known about it. All he ever did was to be active in the Japanese Community Center. That's certainly not a reason for being picked up!"

"I understand," Bill said patiently. "But you guys have to remember that Japan and the United States have been on a collision course for quite a while. I heard the FBI has already been checking on the Japanese community for years and came up with nothing. They have a file on everyone. Even the JACL was scrutinized and finally verified by the FBI. In fact, there are rumors the FBI has asked the JACL to turn in anyone with pro-Japanese views."

"This doesn't make sense. If the FBI already checked us out, why are all these men being picked up?" asked George. "But on the other hand, if we do have spies, shouldn't they be turned in?"

Mack leaped out of his chair and pounded the table with his fist. "God damn you, George! How can you say that, you jerk," he screamed. "My father isn't a spy, and you know it!"

George looked bewildered. "Hey, wait a second. I didn't call your father a spy. I only—"

Tomi was startled as she watched the exchange between the two men. The gentle, fun-loving Mack she knew was transformed into a stranger full of fury and condemnation.

"Hold it, Mack," Bill intervened. "No one is calling your father a spy. George was just speculating. Take it easy. I don't have all the answers, but we have to keep our heads and not lose sight of our perspectives. Let me try to explain to you what's going on. The reason I'm telling you all this is because I've decided to take a stand in defending our rights. I'll be too busy to keep in touch with any of you for a while."

"Why are you doing this?" asked Tomi fretfully. She resented Bill for knocking the JACL. After all, *he* was the one who was out of step. How could he sit there and criticize his own government? He was rocking the boat.

"Well, for one thing the government is talking about imposing a curfew as well as putting us in camps," Bill explained. "Both restrictions are unconstitutional."

"You know, Bill, you're going to be arrested," warned Mack. "Maybe you'll even get shot for your troubles."

Bill shrugged. "Goes with the territory," he said lightly.

George growled as he ran his hands through his hair. "For Christ's sake, Bill. We're at war with Japan. Do you think the U.S. government gives a damn about our constitutional rights at a time like this? You buck the system now, and we're all going to pay for it. We have to trust the government and cooperate."

"George, I struggled with this for a long time. Our parents had no way of fighting legislation that prevented them from owning land or becoming citizens because they weren't white. But by virtue of our birthright, *we can fight back.*"

"Well, I still think we should go along with them. So I don't know if you're just plain stupid or you think you're being a hero!" George exclaimed.

Tomi saw Bill's eyes twinkle, and a half-smile adorned his lips. "Take your choice!" he chuckled.

Kiku appeared at the door and motioned Tomi to the kitchen where a tray with tea and a plate of *omanju,* a Japanese pastry, were sitting. As Tomi picked up the tray, her mother looked out the window down into the alley and asked, "Are you expecting someone else? That brown car in the alley has passed the house several times."

"No, Mama. Everyone is here."

"I don't like the looks of that car. It's too dark to see who's in it, but I can tell it is two men. They keep looking up at our house. I think they are *hakujins.*" Kiku spoke rapidly in Japanese and looked alarmed.

Tomi glanced out the window and saw the top of the brown car slowly move past the kitchen window. The wheels of the car crunched across the gravel road, spitting small pebbles in its wake. She tightened her grip on the side of the tray as she watched the car turn and disappear at the end of the alley. She rushed into the living room and whispered loudly, "I'm not sure but I think the FBI is watching us! Mama says there's a car that looks suspicious in the alley." She nervously served tea as the men sat stunned at the news.

"God, I hope I haven't led the FBI to your house," Mack said. He slumped back into the chair and closed his eyes as his head fell forward on his chest. Tomi's irritation at Mack melted as she watched him agonize over his fear. She dared not express her feelings in front of everyone. Instead, she placed an *omanju* on a small plate and slipped it in front of him, but he was oblivious to her offering.

"Well," said Bill. "So much for this meeting. We better break it up. No telling what they might do." He hurriedly stuffed his pen into his shirt pocket as he pushed back his chair. There was a flurry of activity as everyone moved away from the table. Both the tea and *omanju* sat untouched.

Mack and Bill crowded into the small kitchen and apologized to Kiku for not accepting her refreshments.

"I understand," murmured Kiku and bowed to them. "Hurry home to your families. You must be there to protect them."

As everyone moved into the parlor, George stepped to the window and cautiously peeked through the lace curtain. The brown car was sitting directly in front of the house with the motor running. "What do we do now?" he asked.

"Just act normal," Bill answered. "We aren't doing anything wrong."

Tomi was angry and frightened. We never should have met here tonight, she thought. The FBI probably thinks we're all spies. What if all of us are arrested? Maybe they're after Bill. After all, *he's* the troublemaker. Tomi wrapped her arms around herself tightly as the chilling thoughts ran through her mind.

The warmth of the noisy heater shielded the two occupants of the car from the cold, damp air. FBI Agent Keith Armstrong glanced over at his passenger to size him up. He watched from the corner of his eyes as Deputy Albert Cole of the Sheriff's Department lit a cigarette and a gentle wisp of smoke drifted across his face. Armstrong wasn't sure this young deputy would be of any help to him today.

"Now, you're going to have to fill me in on this guy…uh, Saburo Inouye, before we go in. Are we picking him up?" Cole asked as he checked his assignment sheet.

Armstrong pulled a worn briefcase from behind the driver's

seat and sighed as he took out a surveillance report. "The truth is he's clean. Look at this report yourself."

"Okay, Armstrong, don't give me that!" exclaimed Cole. "The FBI wouldn't be wasting their time on a witch hunt. What's this all about?"

"I'm serious. Actually, this raid was set up. Look, I've been with the bureau for a long time. You gotta keep your eyes and ears open so you know what's going on." The agent was silent for a moment and then continued, "The FBI has been checking out this community for years and found nothing to substantiate any subversive activity. Hell, there's even a report made by Munson at the State Department and one by Ringle at Naval Intelligence. They came up with similar findings reaffirming the loyalty of the Japanese Americans, but the bigwigs in the Army aren't listening."

"I don't get it," the deputy complained. "Then why are we wasting our time? I wasn't assigned to your department to play games." He was clearly annoyed.

"You've got a lot to learn," said Armstrong as he shifted in his seat. "The truth is, the Army's got a frigging agenda up its craw and the Provost Marshal General has been browbeating the FBI and the Justice Department to have this raid so they can pick up all the leaders in the Japanese community." He jerked his head toward Cole and added, "That's why you're here today. We're short of men. The Army finally got its way in spite of the FBI reports. Its paving the way for a mass evacuation and figures there won't be any problems. Not even from the American-born Japanese. Most of them are just kids…around 18 years old."

A low whistle escaped from Cole. "Didn't think that sort of thing was legal. I know the American Legion and the California Farm Bureau have been pushing for incarceration of the Japanese on the West Coast. But I don't get the connection between them and the Army." He finished his cigarette and flicked the butt out the window.

"It's called hate, son. Pure unadulterated hate. Every one of those groups has its own reason for hating the Japanese. It's politics and mass hysteria at its worst."

"Guess you're right," the deputy agreed. "The newspaper columnists are having a field day too." He rummaged through a pile of newspapers at his feet, pulled one out and scanned the pages. "Look what Westbrook Pegler says: 'The Japanese should be under guard to the last man and woman right now and to hell with *habeas corpus.*' Strong stuff, huh?"

"Well, I guess it's no skin off my hide," said Armstrong in a weary voice. "This is wartime. People say and do crazy things. Anyway, we got a job to do."

"Oh! Like, ours is not to question why; ours is just to do or die," Cole answered sarcastically.

"Something like that. Come on, let's get this over with." He tugged at the brim of his hat and turned off the motor. Both men got out of the car and made their way up the long wooden stairs leading to Saburo Inouye's home.

From the second floor of his house, Saburo could feel hurried footsteps on the stairway. Just as he opened the bedroom door, George burst in. "Papa, the FBI is here! What shall we do?"

"I know," said Saburo grimly. "I saw them from the window. I will handle this. Did your friends leave? Where is everyone?" he asked in a tight, low voice. "Hurry, we must go downstairs."

George flung his answer over his shoulder as he turned to run down the stairs. "Everyone is in the living room."

Just as Saburo reached the bottom of the stairs, he heard a loud knock on the front door. George stood frozen on the spot. The high window panel on the door was foggy from the warmth of the house, but Saburo could make out the outline of two hats. He put his hand on the doorknob and hesitated. The knocking became more insistent. Tomi quietly slipped into the hallway behind George as Kiku moved close to her husband. Saburo saw

Mack and Bill through the crack in the sliding door and motioned them to stay put. Finally, Saburo pulled open the front door and heard a loud, deep voice say, "Mr. Saburo Inouye? FBI." Armstrong flashed his badge at Saburo and George as he pushed his way into the house.

Tomi grabbed the back of George's sweater and peered from behind at the two men. Deputy Cole spotted her and leaned forward. "Don't worry, young lady, we're not here to hurt you," he said gently. She quickly bobbed her head behind George. Tomi's fright was mixed with resentment as she watched the large frames of the two agents fill the small hallway. Her father and brother were dwarfed in contrast. Look at these *hakujins,* she thought. What right do they have to come here and upset everyone?

Saburo stood with his feet planted firmly apart. "What you want?" he asked Armstrong in halting English.

"Now, don't get upset, pops," said the FBI agent solicitously. "Just here to ask a few questions." His eyes scrutinized every detail in the house as he spoke.

Cole edged himself into the living room and apprehended Bill and Mack. He corralled them into the adjoining dining room and closed the wooden sliding door behind him.

Armstrong ordered the family to take a seat in the living room and began his inquisition. "Do you have arms or contraband of any sort, such as dynamite or a radio transmitter?"

Saburo's limited knowledge of English made the interrogation painfully slow. George did his best to translate what his father could not understand. As he questioned Saburo, Armstrong moved about the room and methodically checked the bookcase and letters that he found stacked in a box. Tomi could see her father becoming more agitated as the questions kept coming. Saburo knew the agent could not read Japanese and resented this white giant going through his personal belongings.

The agent pushed the brim of his hat back with his pen and

smiled. "Well, that's about it right now," he said. "But I want to check the whole house, if you don't mind."

George glared at the agent and thought to himself, yeah, *as if we had a choice.* The agent slid open the door to the dining room where Mack and Bill were seated at the table with Deputy Cole.

"So, what do you have here, Cole?" asked Armstrong.

The deputy acknowledged his partner with a curt nod as he continued to flip through Bill's papers. "I'm not sure, Armstrong. But our boy here is involved with this JACL organization. Know anything about it?

"Yeah, they're harmless. They were checked out long ago. Let it go."

Bill knew he lucked out. He had brought the JACL brochures as a reference to explain his point of view at the meeting tonight, but his own agenda lay safely on his desk at home. He wasn't ready to show his hand yet.

"I want everyone to take a seat in this room while we check out the whole house, understand?" said Armstrong. He heard a disgruntled chorus of "yeses" as Saburo and his family filed into the crowded room and joined Mack and Bill around the table.

An awkward silence fell over the members of the group as they listened to the agents rummaging through the second floor of the house. No one spoke as they exchanged veiled glances and traced the progress of the two men by their muffled footsteps overhead. The pot of tea was cold and the *omanju* sat untouched. Everyone at the table was apprehensive. They already knew what had happened to Mack's father and were expecting the worst.

Tomi stole a look at her father. He sat rigid in his seat, and the palms of his hands lay open on the table. Although his face showed no emotion, his eyes betrayed his fears. Surely her father would not cave in to the whims of these strangers. He was strong and strict, sometimes even cruel, but he was always there to protect them.

Up on the second floor, Armstrong and Cole conducted an incurious search. "I don't know why we're going through the motion," complained Cole. "You know we're not going to find anything." He poked at some letters on Saburo's desk with his pen.

"Yeah, yeah. I know. This Inouye guy isn't a community leader. He's as clean as a baby's bottom. Let's check out the basement and leave."

Both men lumbered down the steep stairs and went back into the dining room. "Which way to the basement?" demanded Armstrong. George glared at him and jerked his head toward the kitchen. The two men made a cursory inspection of the basement and quickly returned.

"Well, folks," said Armstrong, "sorry to have bothered you." He tipped his hat to Kiku, turned and walked toward the front door. Deputy Cole followed close by.

A look of relief and amazement crossed everyone's faces. The family stood up as one and escorted the two men to the door. Kiku skirted around the two unwelcome visitors and opened the door for them. As the pair made their way down the front steps, a collective sigh of relief escaped from everyone's lips. No one said a word.

Tomi ran to the living room window and watched as the two men got into their car and rattled down the cobblestone street. She silently mouthed the words, "They're gone!" and grabbed George's arm. Her relief knew no bounds. She peered out the window again and saw the curtain in the house across the street move. Tomi knew the Kato family who lived there had been watching the raid. Her friend, Yae Kato, had already told her that her mother had a small duffel bag packed for her father in case the FBI came for him.

Everyone in the room realized how lucky they had been. Most of the families who were raided by the FBI met the fate of Mack's father, whose whereabouts were still unknown, and their houses were left in shambles.

"Huh," said Saburo. "I guess I am not important enough to be picked up." But the relief on his face spoke for itself. "Well, at least you young people are safe." He turned to Mack and Bill and said, "Do not do anything to aggravate the government. This is your country and you must all cooperate and show your loyalty."

"Yes, Mr. Inouye," the two men replied simultaneously like schoolboys.

Bill pulled on his overcoat. After what happened here tonight, it would be counterproductive to try to talk sense into these people, he thought. Might as well go home and lay out some strategy. He would have to be more careful. Tonight was a close call. He paid his respects to Kiku and Saburo and left.

Tomi sidled up to Mack and asked, "Are you all right? I meant to tell you how sorry I am about your father. I hope what happened here tonight didn't upset you too much. It sure scared me." She looked at him anxiously and saw him staring back as if he didn't really see her.

"Yeah, I'm fine. Look, ah…," Mack hesitated a moment before speaking. "I may not be able to come around for a while. With my father gone, my mother will need me. Okay?" He was pleading with his eyes.

"Sure, I understand. Your mother comes first." She returned Mack's glance and tried to look sincere. Tomi knew Mrs. Hara did not approve of her, and she was not happy with Mack's decision to stay away. The warm fuzzy feeling she had for Mack dissipated and was replaced with a feeling of rejection. She walked him to the door and watched him go down the stairs. Mack got into his shiny Ford and drove away.

"Mama's boy," she said under her breath and closed the door.

# 5

## Panic

Tomi slept fitfully through the night. The FBI raid last evening had been terrifying and the cumulative events of the recent days had taken their toll on her nerves. She awoke early to the faint crooning that echoed softly through the quiet morning. It was Joe, the newspaper man. Joe was a big, black man whose smile and gentle manner drew children to him like a magnet. He used to have a newsstand on Jackson Street, and all the children would eye him with curiosity as they walked to and from school. He had a black patch over his right eye and his left sleeve was empty from the elbow down. Sometimes he would sing and do a soft-shoe routine for the children with finesse, and upon finishing, he would throw back his head and roar with laughter. The children were fascinated by him but forbidden to talk to him by fearful mothers who distrusted him because he was a vagrant.

Now he delivered the daily newspaper and serenaded the neighborhood as he covered his route. Tomi could hear his voice rise to a high, melancholic tone that faintly reverberated and gradually faded away. It was comforting to listen to Joe's familiar crooning, and she found solace in its pure simplicity. A sense of normalcy returned for a brief moment.

Tomi was still groggy from lack of sleep but forced herself to get dressed and ready for school. She put on her white middy blouse with a sailor collar and tied a navy blue scarf around her neck. She zipped up her dark blue pleated skirt and ruefully noticed the skimpy pleats that yawned open every time she took a step. She envied her friends who had skirts made with yards of pleats that swished gracefully as they walked. She stepped into her saddle shoes and ran down the stairway.

Her mother appeared in the hallway and shushed her. "Be quiet. Your father is on the phone," Kiku said in a whisper.

Tomi wondered why her father was still home. He usually left for work before 5 a.m. She tiptoed into the living room where Saburo was talking on the phone. He never used the phone unless it was absolutely necessary, so she knew it must be an emergency. She heard him gasp as he pressed the phone to his ear.

*"Nan-da-te?" What did you say?* Saburo said incredulously. She slipped past him and followed her mother into the kitchen. It was obvious from the tone of her father's voice that something was amiss.

"Who is Papa talking to?" Tomi asked her mother.

"It's Mr. Goto. He's having trouble getting his money out of the bank to pay the delivery people. That is why Papa is home today," said Kiku with a worried frown. Saburo had gone to work for Mr. Goto after he lost his own market in the Depression. Tomi wasn't sure what her mother was talking about, but she chose not to question her any further.

The kitchen door flung open, and Saburo started to speak urgently in Japanese to Kiku. He was agitated, and his tone of voice was edged with fear. He spoke so fast Tomi could not understand everything he said, but she caught the drift of the conversation and concluded that Mr. Goto was upset because the government closed his bank account and he could not write a check or get any cash. Mr. Goto told Saburo to take food from the market in place of his wages because he would not be able to keep his market open without money.

Tomi realized that if Mr. Goto was forced to close his market, her father would lose his job, and the family would have very little to live on. George's part-time job paid enough for his school expenses and Kiku's housework jobs were sporadic and her pay meager. Why would the government close Mr. Goto's bank account? None of this was making any sense to her. Tomi excused herself and ran upstairs to tell George about the latest crisis. She banged on his bedroom door and without waiting for an answer she burst into his room. "George! Wake up!" she yelled. "I have to tell you something!"

"Oh, for crying out loud! What do you want?"

Tomi told him about the tense conversation in the kitchen. By the time she finished, George was wide awake and hurried her out of the room so he could get dressed. With his shoes in hand, George raced down the stairs with Tomi close behind him.

"What are you going to do?" asked Tomi.

George answered as he hurried through the living room and picked up the phone.

"Tell Papa that I'm going to call Bill Imada. He's a lawyer. He should know what's going on. I think Mr. Goto misunderstood the people at the bank. I can't imagine the government doing anything that stupid."

Tomi composed herself before entering the kitchen—she knew Kiku would not approve of any show of emotion. She relayed George's message to her parents, and the three of them sat silently at the kitchen table and waited for George to find out what Bill had to say. No one was hungry, and breakfast went untouched. They could hear George's muffled voice through the thin walls as he questioned Bill about the latest debacle.

Finally, George joined the family, and Tomi could tell by the look on his face that the news was not good. He sat across from his parents and tried to speak to them in English and broken Japanese. He struggled to explain to them that the Treasury Department had indeed ordered a blanket shutdown of all bank accounts with Japanese names, and it didn't matter whether they were *issei* or *nisei*.

"So, Mr. Goto was right. The government did shut down his account," George told his father. "That's the reason all the suppliers and delivery truck drivers will not bring Mr. Goto his vegetables and meat unless he pays them cash. Not only that, but Bill told me that the federal agents are starting to close down some businesses on Jackson Street. I have no idea why."

"How are we going to eat?" asked Kiku. She knew they had already extended their credit at the corner grocery store and could not ask for more. They had been living from paycheck to paycheck and did not have any money in the bank as a cushion.

"I don't know," said Saburo. "The rent is due a week after Christmas. That's only two weeks from now. If I am not working, I can't pay the rent either."

"Well, I hear welfare is available but—" George began to speak but was cut off by Saburo.

"I will *never* go on welfare! How dare you suggest such a stupid thing!" Their father was fuming with anger and pounded the table with his fist, sending the dishes crashing to the floor.

"Papa, listen to me," said George, trying to pacify him. "I'm trying to tell you that according to Bill, Mas Aoki, who is one of the leaders in the JACL, is going to contact Senator Thompson in Washington, D.C., today to put a stop to these senseless restrictions. We have to be patient. If anyone can do something, it's Mas. It's just going to take a while." Although George spoke in English, Saburo understood him and could not restrain his emotions.

"I don't see how that is going to help us now," he said grimly.

Just at that moment, there was an urgent knock on the kitchen door, and Tomi saw Mr. Goto's anxious face pressed against the kitchen window as he shaded his eyes. She opened the door, and Mr. Goto rushed in without greeting the family in the traditional manner. He spoke directly to Saburo and ignored everyone else.

"Saburo, hurry—you must come at once! We still have time to open the market today. My wife had some cash hidden away, so I can manage for a couple of days. Come, let's go!" Mr. Goto was a few years younger than Saburo, and his high energy matched his impulsive nature. He stepped over the broken dishes and grabbed Saburo by the arm. Both men hurried out the door to the alley below as Kiku bid them goodbye. They heard Mr. Goto spinning the wheels of his rickety truck on the gravel as he took off with Saburo in tow.

Tomi was confused. Everything was happening too fast; she did not have time to sort it out. She felt overburdened and tried to block everything out. She gathered her books and got ready to leave for school. George was on the phone again, trying to get more information from the JACL office while Kiku cleaned up the kitchen.

As Tomi left her house, she saw Yae Kato coming out of her house across the street. They used to play together occasionally when they were youngsters, but the girls drifted apart when Tomi started high school several years ago. Yae was petite and thin. Her complexion was darker than Tomi's, but it only enhanced her dark brown eyes and long, thick lashes. She was usually very congenial and talkative, but today she looked distracted and worried. Tomi waved to Yae and hurried over to her.

"Did you hear what happened to Mr. Goto?" asked Tomi. She proceeded to tell Yae the events of the morning at her house.

"Ours is worse than that," said Yae. "A couple of federal agents came to my father's drugstore yesterday afternoon and closed it down."

"I can't believe that!" exclaimed Tomi. "Why?"

"I don't know. Oh yeah, not only that, but they barged in and took all the money and some other stuff and locked it all up in the safe. He couldn't even pay his workers." She fought to hold back her tears.

The two girls sat on the front porch as Yae told how her father tried to get the agents to let him put things in order and clean up but they wouldn't allow him to do anything.

"My father said he even tried to call the federal authorities to find out what was going on but he didn't have any luck. Then the agents put a padlock on the front of the store with some kind of sign and told him to leave. So, Papa couldn't do anything else but go home."

Tomi hastened to tell Yae what George had said about the JACL getting in touch with Senator Thompson in Washington, D.C., to stop these shutdowns by the federal agents. She was hoping the news would cheer her up.

"I sure hope George is right," said Yae, shaking her head. Tomi could tell by the tone of her voice that she was not optimistic.

Yae's mother cracked open the front door and reminded the girls that they would be late for school. "No matter what is going on with your father, you must go to school," she chided Yae.

The two girls walked up the hill without talking. Both were emotionally spent and further discussion seemed useless. When they reached Parkland High School, the tardy bell was ringing. Yae dashed to her class so she wouldn't be late, but Tomi took her time entering her home room and slid into a seat unnoticed. School was getting less and less important to her on a daily basis. Miss Sidney was busy writing the assignments on the board. The sound of pencils scratching on paper took over the silence of the room and another school day began. Christmas vacation was less than a week away. Tomi knew that Christmas would be bleak, but she was looking forward to staying home and doing nothing.

Over the next few days, Mr. Goto and Saburo struggled frantically to keep the market going on a shoestring and meet the demands of the creditors as well as the customers. Yae's father was not as fortunate and became more distressed when he learned that his car insurance was also canceled for no apparent reason. It was one more blow for him. He had no control over the whims of the creditors or the government, and the prospect of losing a lucrative business was devastating.

\* \* \*

Four days after the Treasury Department froze the bank accounts of all Japanese as well as the accounts in local branches of Japanese banks, the government decided to allow the people to withdraw up to $100 a month for living expenses. Concurrently, the closures of the businesses were halted, and many of the stores that had been shut down were allowed to reopen. No one knew how or why these changes were made and if, in fact, Senator Thompson was able to persuade the Treasury Department to soften its ruling. No one really cared. Most businessmen were trying to carry on with crippled bank accounts and recoup their losses. The whole community was reeling from the effects of the upheavals.

Yae's father reopened his drugstore, and he was thankful that there was still time for Christmas shoppers to come to his store. As for Mr. Goto's problems, they were far from over but the $100 a month eased his shortage of cash, and Saburo was able to keep his job and feed his family.

Tomi and Yae felt a huge relief after the stressful episode. They renewed their friendship by going to the Pioneer Bakery for a chocolate Hostess cupcake.

# 6

## Broken Curfew

After Christmas vacation, Tomi returned to school and noticed a change in the attitude of the students. What started out as benign acceptance of the young *nisei* students was gradually ebbing, and an air of tension began to build daily. Tomi felt herself withdrawing from the Caucasian students and spoke only with her Japanese friends. She avoided contact with all the teachers whenever possible. As much as she admired Miss Sidney, Tomi felt uncomfortable in her presence. She knew she was no longer attuned to academic studies and was not even concerned. Tomi felt she was letting Miss Sidney down, though, and rather than face her, she started skipping classes. Although most of her friends studied diligently and continued to accelerate academically, Tomi's scholastic standing was nose-diving. Well, who cares, she thought. The way things were going, nothing mattered anymore. The class forged ahead as Tomi fell more and more behind.

One day Tomi saw her friend, Beverly Friedman, in the gym. Tomi was fond of Beverly. They had known each other since kindergarten, and she was one of the few *hakujin* friends Tomi had.

Beverly was gregarious and funny and always made her laugh. She had dark brown hair, which curled into long ringlets, in stark contrast to her pinkish-white skin. "Where have you been hiding?" she squealed.

"Oh, I've been skipping class," replied Tomi, grinning.

Beverly looked at Tomi inquisitively. "Why? I know you don't like school, but this doesn't sound like you. You never do things like that. Now, me, yeah!" she said and let out a howl.

"Haven't you been reading the newspaper? All you read about is how the Japanese Americans are spies and not loyal to America. Now they want to put us all in some kind of camp. Even the radio is full of that stuff. So why should I care about going to school?"

Beverly became serious. "Don't worry, Tomi. My dad says these are just wild rumors and the government will never put you in camps. It's just talk. You're an American citizen." She spread her hands wide and added, "They can't do it."

"Hope your dad is right," said Tomi as Beverly rushed off.

* * *

George continued his classes at the university and made it a point to stay closer to home after the war began. Lately, he had been noticing Tomi coming home early from school. "Are you skipping school?" he asked one day.

"Yeah, so what's it to you?" Tomi said defiantly. "I hate that stupid high school."

"It's *you* that's stupid. When Papa finds out, you're really in for it."

"There's nothing going on. Besides, I can't concentrate. Are you going to snitch?"

George looked at his sister for a moment. He was aware of Tomi's frustration and knew this was not the time to tease her.

"No, I'm not. They got enough on their minds. Look, Tomi. Things have been pretty hairy around here, but it's going to get worse. If you don't straighten out and hang in there, you're not going to make it. Did you see today's paper?" He handed her the front page of the *PI*.

Tomi glanced at the headline that screamed, "Curfew Imposed on Japs: 8 p.m. to 6 a.m."

"Ye gads, what next," she moaned.

"See? That means I won't have a night job at Walgreens anymore. You're not the only one going through this, you know."

Tomi flopped into Saburo's oversized chair. She knew George was right. This was one of the rare times her brother had bothered to talk to her, and she was pleased and flattered at his attention.

"Okay, I'll try to stay in school," she said.

"You will *what?*"

"Okay, okay. I *will* stay in school."

"Good!"

"Jeez," she mumbled.

The phone rang, and George answered. It was Bill Imada.

"George! Did you see the *PI?* This is what I've been waiting for. Now I'll be able to test our constitutional rights by challenging this new curfew law. In fact, I've arranged to do it tonight, but I need your help. I can't ask Mack because he's dead set against my plans." Bill sounded excited.

"You're crazy, Bill! You're only one person. I think Mack is right. What can you do? No one is backing you, you know."

Bill ignored his protest and continued. "I've already notified the FBI and the U.S. Attorney of my intentions, and I need you to get in touch with my friend, Bruce White. He agreed to track my progress and keep the FBI informed of my whereabouts. I don't want you or Tomi involved because it might get dangerous. Call Bruce and tell him I'll meet him on 14th and Spruce Street at 8:30 tonight." Bill spoke rapidly and decisively and hung up.

"Damn him, anyhow," swore George. "He's going to get himself killed." He turned to Tomi and said, "Bill's going to carry out his crazy scheme tonight. I'm not even going to call Bruce. I better go down and try and stop him."

"I'll go with you, George," said Tomi. "Better let Mack know. Maybe the three of us can change his mind."

"*You* call Mack."

"I'm not talking to him."

"Again? Why don't you grow up?" he said and picked up the phone. He reached Mack and told him of Bill's plan. Mack quickly agreed to pick them up at 7:30.

\* \* \*

Tomi had not seen much of Mack since the FBI raid. He had stopped by at Christmas for a visit, but her attraction to him was beginning to wane. As much as she sympathized with him on the unknown fate of his father, his constant complaining of the government's treachery was beginning to grate on her nerves.

When Mack arrived to pick them up, Tomi sat next to him in the front seat and George squeezed in next to her.

"And how's your mother, Mack?" asked Tomi in a mocking voice. George elbowed her sharply, but Mack was too preoccupied to notice.

"She's fine," answered Mack absently. "But I'm worried about Bill. How are we going to get him out of there? It's almost our 8 o'clock curfew now. Man, he's persistent. We have to stop him."

Mack floored the accelerator and sped up the hill. As the car approached Spruce Street, they could see Bill pacing nervously. He recognized Mack's car and waved for him to stop.

"What are you guys doing here?" Bill demanded. "Don't you know it's almost curfew time? Go on home!"

"Not until you do," answered Mack. "Come on, Bill, give it up. You can't win. There's no point to this."

Bill peered into the car and saw Tomi. "Why did you bring her, Mack? She's a girl. You know there might be trouble," he scolded.

Bill didn't want her on his conscience if they were all arrested.

"Forget that. She's already here. It's you we're worried about." Mack was getting irritated at Bill. How could he be so reckless? Yet, as foolhardy as Bill was, Mack secretly admired him for taking a stand.

Tomi and George got out of the car. "Come on, Bill," she said, "go home. We don't want you to get into trouble."

"There's no point in belaboring the issue, Tomi. This is a matter of principle." Bill pushed his chest out and stood with his arms rigid at his sides.

Tomi almost giggled and hid her mouth behind her hands. She thought he looked like a short samurai. Why is Bill making all this fuss about breaking curfew, she wondered. It doesn't make any sense. Tomi looked at her watch, and it read 8:20 p.m. They were already in violation, and it was starting to make her nervous. Her family had already lucked out with the FBI a couple of weeks ago, but she wasn't sure what would happen today. Suddenly, she saw a car approaching with a police officer behind the wheel. "Hey, you guys, jiggers," she warned. "There's a police car coming. Let's get out of here!"

"Too late," said George. "He spotted us. Stay where you are."

George looked worried. He suddenly realized what a mistake it was to bring Tomi. She's just a kid yet, he thought. What was I thinking? Bill was right. Too late now.

The police officer slowed down and poked his head out the window. "What is this? A convention?" he asked laughingly and got out of the patrol car.

Tomi heard Bill moan softly. "Oh no! It's Mr. Goodman. That's all I need."

Sam Goodman and his family had lived next door to the Imada family for years. His son, Chuck, and Bill grew up together until the Goodmans moved away. Gradually, the boys lost contact as they went their separate ways. Sam was a big, jovial man who fit the role of a congenial police officer to whom little children flocked. He had been like a second father to Bill when he was young.

Sam was the last person Bill wanted to see. He knew Sam would never go along with his plans to be arrested. It was bad enough having to contend with his three unwelcome but well-meaning friends.

Sam stared hard at Bill for a moment. He bent his rotund body slightly forward, and with his hands resting lightly on his knees he said, "Well, I'll be darned! Is that you, Bill? How are you? Wait 'til I tell mama I saw you. But what are you and your friends doing out here? Don't you know there's a curfew?" Sam was incredulous to find his young friend standing in the middle of the street at this hour.

"Hello, Mr. Goodman," Bill said with a heavy sigh. Before Sam could ask any more questions, a frenzy of words tumbled out and he bombarded Sam with every detail of his plans.

As he listened to Bill, Sam's pleasant face took on a stern expression, and he finally interrupted the young man. "Enough of this nonsense! If I arrest you, I'm taking the whole lot of you in—even the girl!" Sam knew Bill would never let his friends be arrested.

It was clear to Tomi and everyone there that Sam Goodman was not going to allow Bill to carry out his plans. Suddenly, she sprinted across the street in reckless abandonment and stood by the sign posted on the telephone pole that read,

MILITARY ZONE. Off limits to Japs.

"Look! I'm in the off-limit zone!" she yelled and twirled around the pole.

Sam was not amused. "Get back here, young lady—you ought to be spanked." Turning to George, he said, "Hey, you! Get her back here! I want all of you to get in that car and go home." Sam pointed his nightstick at Mack's car as he spoke. "And you!" he said, pointing at Bill, "Get in my car! I'm taking you home."

Bill protested. "But you don't understand the significance of this—"

"I don't want to hear another word out of you," said Sam. His face was red and angry.

He could not believe Bill Imada would lay his life on the line for such a foolish cause. Sam knew the only way he could protect his young, foolhardy friend was to take him home. Tomi was surprised to see Bill draw his small stature up as tall as he could to confront Sam.

"I'm not going," said Bill firmly as he stood with his legs apart, toe-to-toe with the big man.

Before Bill could say or do anything, Sam whirled him around with one swoop of his large hand and marched him by the cuff of his coat collar to the patrol car like an errant child. He opened the door and threw Bill into the front seat and slammed the door.

"There! Now stay there," he growled. Sam put both hands on his hips and shook his head. "Mother of Jesus. What I have to put up with," he mumbled under his breath. "Wait 'til Mrs. Goodman hears what you're up to," he said, shaking his fingers at Bill.

George and Mack leaned against the Ford and watched Bill, the lawyer, being reprimanded like a small child. Both men had wide grins on their faces as they folded their arms across their chests. They were trying hard not to laugh and dropped their heads to hide their mirth. They knew Bill was not going to jail tonight.

Tomi was not as diplomatic and giggled out loud. She was not unhappy to see Bill humiliated. Maybe now he'll simmer down and stop this nonsense, she thought.

Sam heard her giggle. He spun around and commanded, "As for *you* three, I told you to get out of here! Now GO!"

As Mack pulled away from the patrol car, they could see Bill slumped in the front seat, looking sheepish. They could hear Sam scolding poor Bill as Mack deliberately drove slowly by.

"…And furthermore…," Sam was yelling, and everyone in Mack's car broke out in laughter. All the way home they mimicked the officer's tirade. They were grateful and relieved Bill was safe, but they also enjoyed watching their friend eat humble pie.

Later that evening, Bill again notified the FBI of his intentions. He slipped out of his house unnoticed and turned himself in to the First Precinct headquarters. Bill Imada finally accomplished what he had set out to do. He was arrested for violating the curfew law.

# 7

## Betrayed

It was mid-February 1942. A three-inch glaring headline in the *Seattle Post-Intelligencer* read,

"ALL JAPS TO BE EVACUATED IMMEDIATELY!"

Tomi was stunned when she saw the news. She never dreamed it would happen. Moreover, the one person she had counted on had betrayed her. She never thought her President, Franklin Delano Roosevelt, would be part of such a plan. She had seen his kindly face many times on "Eyes of the World" newsreels in the movie-house with his elegant clip-on glasses perched on his aristocratic nose and an elegant, slender cigarette holder dangling from his lips. But there he was on the front page of the *PI*. The President was signing Executive Order 9066 to evacuate all alien Japanese and Japanese Americans living on the West Coast to internment camps. How could he do that?

Her whole world came crashing down. The cocoon she wrapped around herself in recent weeks had given her a false sense of security, and now it was ripped apart. She was bitterly disappointed and frightened by the turn of events. The rage she felt began to smolder and fester, but it had nowhere to go. In the end, she smothered her feelings and accepted the inevitable, as did her friends and family.

"*Gaman yo!*" said her mother. *You must endure!*

"They're giving us two weeks to get ready to leave," George announced after reading the article.

"Two weeks! We can't get ready that soon," wailed Tomi. "How are we going to get rid of everything? How about my piano?"

"*Our* piano," corrected George.

"Oh, who cares? You know what I mean."

"Stop your whining, Tomi, and start packing," her mother scolded. "The Baptist Church will allow us to store some things on their property and we can sell the big items, like the piano," she said without looking at Tomi.

"What?" said Tomi in disbelief. How could her mother think of doing such a foolish thing? But she didn't dare challenge her mother to her face; that wouldn't be proper.

Tomi's love for music was born out of loneliness. When the house was empty, she would play the piano to escape into another world where she could express her feelings through music.

She had admired Alice Uno from the day she started taking piano lessons from her five years ago. Alice's gentleness and patience helped accelerate Tomi's musical progress. She taught piano while she worked on her degree in sociology at the University of Washington.

Tomi loved to go to the wooden house where Alice lived. It was a large, two-story house. She had never seen a lovelier home except for those where her mother worked. She would count the 12 steps leading up to the white porch that stretched across the front. The music room was Tomi's favorite. There were two black grand pianos, which were placed back to back in the spacious studio.

Occasionally, Alice would accompany Tomi on one piano while

Tomi played the melody on the other. Together they would finish the piece with Alice adding a crescendo of chords, which made the room resound with the rich, vibrant music.

"There," Alice would say. "*This* is the way I want you to learn to play."

Tomi never forgot the overwhelming pure joy as music flowed from both pianos. Music was the sanctuary in which she found solace. It was the one place where her spirit could soar into another dimension and set her free from the harsh reality of the world.

Tomi soon found that her mother had her own ideas concerning the piano. Kiku put out word that the piano was for sale for $25. A private school offered to buy the magnificent Baldwin upright grand piano. Two men and a woman came to check out the piano and close the deal. As soon as the trio arrived, Kiku invited them into the living room where they sat gingerly on the edge of their chairs, looking very uncomfortable. Tomi sensed their uneasiness and prayed her mother would not ask her to play. With a hard smile Kiku said to the trio, "My daughter, she play for you now," and motioned Tomi to the piano. All three declined the offer and murmured some feeble excuses, but Kiku insisted her daughter play for the guests. Tomi and the trio reluctantly shared five agonizing minutes of unsolicited classical music while Kiku stood beaming the whole time. She knew the trio would never forget that experience. Nor did Tomi.

When the door closed on the three visitors, Kiku crossed her arms across her chest and said, "Huh!"

* * *

The frantic pace to meet "E-Day" (Evacuation Day) quickened. Tomi had no time to stay depressed for very long. There was less than a week to go. Huge posters with instructions to the evacuees were hammered on telephone poles and posted on bulletin boards. The house was a shambles, with clothing and furniture scattered in disarray. It was a race against time. Everyone worked feverishly to get things in order.

"Do you know that last bulletin said we could only take what we can carry?" Tomi asked her father.

"Do not be foolish," said Saburo. "How can we manage to survive on what we can carry? You must be mistaken."

"No, Papa. Here, I have a copy of the instructions. See?" she said, handing him the sheet of paper.

"You know I cannot read all that complicated English writing," he scolded. "Read it and translate it properly."

"Yes, Papa. It says exactly what I told you. Only one suitcase per person and whatever you can carry."

"Not only that," George added, "it says every member of the family must be registered at the Control Center."

"Very well, George," said Saburo. "You will go with me now to register."

* * *

When George and Saburo came back from the Control Center, Tomi noticed her father's grim expression. George was visibly angry and slammed the front door as he entered.

"Look!" he yelled, shaking 20 long white tags. "Look at these dumb tags. You know what it says? Nothing! No name, just numbers. We are now Family #17337. Not only that, we have to *wear* these tags just like our baggage."

Tomi looked at the numbered tags and felt a shocking wave of humiliation and disgrace wash over her. This was the last straw. She was no longer a person; she was a number. The rage within her was rekindled. Tomi promised herself that someday she would show the world she was somebody. I'll show them, she thought. *I'll show them!*

Meanwhile, Kiku kept packing as she listened to George's outburst. "We will have to do the best we can with what we have.

There is no other way. *Shikata ga nai,*" said Kiku. "It can't be helped. Now, stop complaining about those tags and help me pack. *Gaman yo!*"

Saburo scowled but said nothing. Tomi knew her father was working up a tirade to vent his frustration, and she quickly escaped to her room. As she rummaged through her belongings, her eyes drifted across the room and rested on a beautiful Japanese doll dressed in silk brocade. It was enclosed in a glass case edged with a thin, black lacquered frame. The exquisite porcelain face was offset by a jet-black wig and miniature silver hair jewelry. Tomi wondered who would keep the doll for her until she returned to Seattle again. She decided to ask Mrs. Alice Hill. Tomi occasionally babysat for the Hills on weekends. She carefully put the encased doll into a specially made wooden box. She would take it with her this weekend to the Hills to explain why she would not be back to babysit.

Saturday arrived, and Tomi took the bus to Mrs. Hill's home. As soon as she arrived, she knew something was wrong. The blinds in the house were lowered and there was no sign of the usual hustle and bustle of daily life. The children, Nick and Sue, were nowhere to be seen. She knocked on the door, but no one answered. Tomi knocked harder, and finally Alice Hill opened the door a crack.

"Hello, Tomi," she said softly, almost whispering.

"Hello, Mrs. Hill. I just came by to tell you I won't be back after today. We're going to be evacuated."

"Yes, I know. I read about it in the *PI*. I am so sorry."

Tomi was surprised to hear Alice apologize. Why should she be sorry? No one else was.

"By the way, Tomi, I don't need you tonight," she said and glanced at the large wooden box Tomi was carrying.

"That's okay. I really don't have time anyway. But I have to ask you something. Could you please keep this doll for me until I come back?" Tomi extended the box toward her.

Alice opened the door a little wider. "Oh, no. I can't," she said as she pushed the box away.

Tomi took a deep breath and said, "It's a Japanese doll my uncle sent to me many years ago from Japan. Please, Mrs. Hill," begged Tomi, "I have no place to leave it."

"You don't understand, Tomi. Several of my neighbors work for the FBI, and if they see you here, I don't know what they will do. You have to leave. I'm sorry." Alice spoke rapidly and ran her words together. Tomi could see that she was very frightened.

"But, Mrs. Hill, you know me. I've worked for you. I'm not a spy or anything. You know that."

"Yes! Yes! I know, but you have to leave now. Just leave that box on the porch. I'll...take care of it later. Bye, Tomi," said Alice in a low voice, and she softly closed the door.

Tomi was hurt and bewildered. She had come to this house many times to babysit and suddenly she was no longer welcome. Mrs. Hill's behavior puzzled Tomi. She felt abandoned. Tomi walked away from the house and turned to see the outline of the delicate, light wood-grained box sitting on the porch, discarded. She remembered Mrs. Hill's warning about the FBI, and Tomi could almost feel unseen eyes following her to the bus stop. She knew one thing for certain—she would never see her doll again. Tomi boarded the bus with a heavy heart. As she sank into her seat, she was overwhelmed with sadness. Someone from the back of the bus mumbled, "Jap!" She felt herself cringe inside but sat staring straight ahead until she got to her stop.

Tomi climbed the hill to her house and just as she walked into the kitchen, George appeared and asked, "Where've you been? I've been looking all over for you. The JACL is having another emergency meeting at the Nippon Kan this afternoon, so I think we better go."

Tomi was still feeling the sting of rejection and could only nod in agreement. George noticed her pensive mood.

"What's wrong? Mack again, huh?" he teased.

"No, I just got back from Mrs. Hill's house." Tomi proceeded to explain to George what happened. "I still don't get it. I didn't do anything wrong," she insisted.

"Hey, it's only a doll," said George lightly.

"You know it's more than the doll, George."

"Yeah, a lot more," he said grimly. Neither said a word for a while. There was an uneasy silence between the siblings, as they struggled with their own feelings. Finally George spoke.

"By the way, Mack called and said he would pick us up."

"You mean he's *really* coming?" asked Tomi in a mocking tone.

"What's with you two, anyhow?"

"Well, he's always catering to his mother and, besides, she hates me."

"Ignore her," said George.

"I can't. Whenever she sees me, she gives me a dirty look."

"Well, did you know Papa doesn't like you going with Mack? He thinks you're too young to be going around with him. He told me to tell you."

"What do you think of Mack, George?"

"I like him. Give him a chance. He's a nice guy."

"Hmm," she murmured. "We'll see."

"God, you're a brat."

"Uh huh," she replied.

# 8

## Ghost Town

Tomi heard Mack's Ford rattle to a stop in front of the house. She watched him from the living room window as he bounded up the steps. Tomi opened the door and shyly greeted him. As usual, he had brought her a small gift. It was a pen.

"Just in case we get sent to different camps, you can write to me." Mack cocked his head. "You're awfully quiet. You okay?"

Tomi was grateful for his concern and poured out her feelings about Executive Order 9066 and her ordeal with Mrs. Hill.

Mack listened compassionately and allowed her to vent her anger until she was spent. He moved toward her but stopped short of embracing her. Instead, he put both hands on her shoulders and said, "I know how you feel, Tomi. But I don't know the answer to all this mess. Maybe we'll find out something tonight at the meeting." Mack released her shoulders and cupped her face gently. Tomi turned quickly away, but she was touched and comforted by Mack's sensitivity.

\* \* \*

On the way to the Nippon Kan, Mack drove to *Nihonmachi* (Japanese Town) with Tomi and George. They were not prepared for the sight that greeted them. They were shocked to see almost all of the stores and restaurants on Jackson Street boarded up. Mack slowed down and finally stopped. There were a few people scattered about, but an ominous silence had descended on Jackson Street. It was a shadow of what was once a bustling business mecca, packed with people and activities. The three stared speechlessly at the sight. Jackson Street, the hub of *Nihonmachi*, was almost deserted. It had become a ghost town.

"Damn," said George, "look at that." A low whistle escaped from his lips.

"Sure gives you the willies," said Tomi. She noticed Jim's Grill was not boarded up. The sign, *Closed,* was posted on the door, but there was a larger sign on the front window that read,

UNDER NEW MANAGEMENT
WHITE AMERICANS
WILL OPEN SOON

She spotted several other stores down Jackson Street with similar signs.

Tomi looked for the grocery store that belonged to an old family friend, Masa Iida. She finally glimpsed a battered canvas sign reading *Oriental Grocery* fluttering above the boarded window. She noticed George taking in the same sight, and without exchanging a word, they shared a feeling of desecration of their friend's store.

Masa was a gentle giant. His large frame and scraggly beard looked out of place among his short, clean-shaven friends, but everyone was charmed by his sunny disposition and gentle manner. Tomi remembered how she and George would look forward to visiting the store when she was about 4 years old. They called Masa,

*Oji-chan* (Uncle), and Hatsue, *Oba-chan* (Auntie). Hatsue was not married to Masa, and Kiku disapproved of their impropriety, but Saburo brushed aside their relationship as a minor infraction. In his eyes, Masa was a man's man—big, strong and successful. Tomi remembered how Saburo timed their visits to the store at closing time. Tomi and George waited patiently until the last customer left, and Masa would carefully pull out a large Baby Ruth bar in a red wrapper or a Butterfinger bar in its bright yellow wrapper from the candy counter and present it to them with exaggerated formality and a twinkle in his eyes. It was a ritual of which she and George never tired.

The small store was crammed with a variety of dry and fresh food, fruits, vegetables, candy, toys and hundreds of other miscellaneous items. Tomi used to watch *Oji-chan* skillfully maneuver his large frame around the small store and as young as she was, she marveled at his agility. Every nook and cranny was filled with mysterious items that were stacked to the ceiling. It was a wonderland for a small, curious child. The best part of the visit was after dinner.

The store was also Masa and Hatsue's home. There were steep wooden stairs that led up to a loft above the store where the living quarters were located. The stairway led into a tiny kitchen crammed with a stove, icebox and a low table. Outside the kitchen a small wooden porch held an array of Hatsue's plants that spilled onto a stairway and zigzagged down to the alley. Several light bulbs hung from the low ceiling of the kitchen. Once seated, no one could move without stepping over one another Tomi was fascinated with the small Oriental figurines that occupied every inch of a wooden buffet, which was jammed into a corner of the kitchen. After dinner, Tomi and George would succumb to the warmth of the small room and a full stomach.

Several *shoji* screens separated the kitchen from the sleeping area where Hatsue kept several full-size *futons* (quilts) piled on the straw mat. The sleeping area had a high wooden railing that provided a bird's-eye view of the store. Hatsue would lay out the *futons* on the straw mat for Tomi and George after dinner. Tomi remembered being gently tucked in by Hatsue. The murmur of the adults' voices and bursts of laughter mixed with the warm air would lull her into a deep, contented sleep. In spite of its glaring deficiencies, Oriental Grocery was a cherished haven for Tomi and George.

Mack drove slowly down Jackson Street, as the three continued to view the devastation.

"Look," said George. "Somebody bought Mr. Kawakami's hotel." A huge sign stretched across the front window read, *New Management.* Tomi remembered as a toddler being scolded by Kiku for trying to aim her spit in the brass spittoon. The residents at the hotel did it with such accuracy and skill.

The signs on the flower shop and Mori's 10-Cent Store were still visible on the buildings, but the doors and windows were boarded up.

Mack turned the corner on 6th Street and moved slowly up the steep hill.

Halfway up the hill, Tomi saw parts of a vertical sign through the slits of a boarded building. She knew the sign read *Furo.* Saburo used to take the whole family to the bathhouse on Saturday nights before visiting the Iidas.

Mack drove several more blocks to Maynard and turned into the Nippon Kan parking lot, which was filled to capacity. Tomi noticed most of the people streaming into the building were *nisei* and only a few were *issei.* It was then that she realized most of the *issei* leaders had already been picked up by the FBI.

# 9

## Opposing Stance

The auditorium was jampacked with people. Tomi managed to find two seats in the back of the room. George joined others already lined up on both sides of the hall. The noise of the crowd intensified as the people streamed in. Finally, Tomi heard Jack Mori, the JACL president, trying to call the meeting to order. It took him several attempts before the crowd responded to his plea to quiet down. He struck the podium repeatedly with his gavel until order was restored. She noticed that Jack's suit looked rumpled and his tie slightly askew. He wasted no time in getting to his message.

"This coming Monday will be the beginning of a new life for all of us. This is the day evacuation will begin for the Seattle area. The JACL has done what they could to help the community to get ready and will continue to expend their efforts to make this transition as painless as possible," he continued. "You have all received your instructions concerning the date of departure as well as the pickup points for you and your baggage."

As Jack continued to give more instructions, Tomi's eyes wandered around the hall, and she thought she saw Bill Imada's profile as she looked toward the front of the auditorium. Couldn't be, she thought. Bill was in jail; he had turned himself in to the police. Tomi turned her attention back to Jack. He took a sip of water from a small glass, cleared his throat and continued to speak.

"The JACL has been meeting with many of the government officials in regard to the evacuation. As you know, the Army has declared the evacuation of the *nisei* and *issei* a military necessity. However, they have promised us the move will be a temporary arrangement, especially the assembly center at Puyallup where everyone will be sent to first."

Jack went on: "The government's main concern is our welfare and protection and they have promised to do everything in their power to carry out the evacuation in a humane manner. We have the assurance of the government officials that everything possible will be done to minimize personal hardships and property losses. For instance, the proceeds from the sale of crops from the farms will be properly accounted for to the farmers who are being evacuated. Therefore, the JACL encourages everyone to cooperate and be of assistance whenever possible."

There was an uneasy pause as a lukewarm applause rippled through the crowd.

Tomi turned to Mack and said, "Jack sure looks tired. I'm not sure I really understand what he means by 'military necessity.' What are we doing that's so bad?"

"According to the Army, we're a bunch of Japanese spies," said Mack.

Tomi shook her head in disbelief. Jack opened the meeting to questions and answers. It was finally adjourned at 6:30 to allow everyone to get home before the 8 p.m. curfew.

Tomi and Mack pushed their way toward the entrance to look for George. They found him waiting near the stairwell with Alice Yoshino, Mack's cousin. Alice was a beautiful girl with almond-shaped eyes. She was Tomi's height and wore her hair curled softly around her face, which set off her perfect features. The two girls greeted each other warmly.

"Who did you come with, Alice?" asked Mack. "You're not alone, are you?"

"No, it's someone I met at a church meeting. Maybe you know him—Bill Imada."

Everyone laughed and answered in unison, "Yeah, we know him!" They were thinking about the incident with Officer Sam Goodman.

Alice looked puzzled and smiled. Just then, Bill appeared.

"Bill!" shouted Mack. He jabbed at him playfully. "I thought you were still in jail."

Bill grinned and greeted everyone. "They let me out on bail."

"Gosh, it's good to see you again!" exclaimed George.

"I thought I saw you in the front. I'm glad to see you're all right," said Tomi. "Did the police treat you okay?"

"Thanks. Those cops at the jail didn't know what to do with me," he said with a smirk.

"So what's going to happen now?" asked Mack.

"Well, I should be going to trial soon. That's what I came to talk to Jack about. I'd like to get the JACL to support me."

Everyone looked uncomfortable. It was common knowledge that the JACL did not approve of what he was trying to do.

"Do you think that's smart, Bill?" asked George.

Bill shrugged his shoulders and smiled. "Don't know 'til I try, right? Look, Jack is waiting for me in Room 4. You guys want to come? I can sure use your support—well, at least your presence."

"Why not," said Tomi, rolling her eyes. "We got you out of one mess already. Maybe we can get you out of this one too."

"You are so funny, Tomi," said Bill, as he tousled her hair.

"Yeah, hilarious," George cut in. "Look, Bill, we know what you're trying to prove, but it's not going to work. The cards are stacked against you."

"Yeah, I know you're right, but you have no idea what's at stake," he warned.

Alice, who was listening quietly, moved toward Bill. She held her arms out to him and said, "I know what you're talking about, Bill. I'll support you. Let's go talk to Jack."

Tomi was surprised at Alice's bold gesture and firm commitment. She heard Bill suck in his breath and his face broke into a huge smile. Without a word he took Alice's hands and pulled her next to him. Everyone exchanged quick glances as if to unanimously confirm the budding relationship. It was obvious that Bill had found more than an advocate.

Bill led the group from the stairwell back into the hallway. As they approached Room 4, they could hear the rapid clicking of a typewriter and the zip of the carriage return responding to the bell. Jack looked up from his typing as everyone crowded into the small room. Sitting next to him was Tosh Mukai, vice president of the JACL, who was sorting out some papers. The two men were surrounded by stacks of books and papers on the shelves, table and floor, some of which were teetering and spilling over.

"Hey, what is this?" Jack said in mock alarm. "I thought you were the only one coming, Bill," he said as he rose to greet everyone. Bill initiated a quick introduction of the group.

There was a ripple of nervous laughter as chairs were shifted around, and Tosh unfolded more chairs to accommodate the crowd. Everyone sat gingerly around the table to avoid setting off an avalanche of paper and books ready to topple on them.

The mood turned serious as Jack reminded everyone that they had an 8 p.m. curfew.

Tomi noticed an air of urgency stemming from Jack. It was clear that his mind was preoccupied. He leaned forward with both arms held stiffly against the table.

"Okay, Bill. What do you want from me?"

"I want the JACL to back me at my trial when it comes up."

Jack drummed his fingers on the table. He lowered his head and shook it vigorously.

"Come on, Bill, you can't be serious," said Jack. "We're in the middle of a crisis and you want the JACL to back *you?*" he asked incredulously. "Let me tell you once and for all what the *real issue* is. I can't go into a lot of detail right now but I gotta tell you that the Army won't stop at anything to put us in camp. You know we've been meeting with government officials to try and stop this madness, but because of the constant bombardment of the press and the politicians, we've been labeled disloyal. You, of all people, should know that the Army would carry out its threat to remove us at gunpoint. Do you want the blood of your *own* people on your head? I don't. We've already been told that if we resist, the Army will consider it an act of treason and won't hesitate to act on it. They have no qualms about carrying out their orders. Is *that* what you want?" Jack slumped back into his chair and stared at Bill.

Tomi was aghast at what she had just heard. Even after Executive Order 9066 was signed, she still had hopes that someone would stop it. This meant on Monday she would be wearing tag #17337. Anger and fright leapfrogged within her, and the painful churning in her stomach made her gasp. George looked at her but did not say anything.

Bill cleared his voice and slid forward to the edge of his chair. "I understand the FBI and the Justice Department never found any incriminating evidence against the *nisei* to substantiate any subversive activities. On that basis alone, I feel our rights are being violated by the executive order. Besides, consider the horrendous economic loss of the people who had to abandon their businesses or sell everything dirt cheap."

Bill studied Jack's face for a moment and said, "Did it ever occur to you that the JACL is being *used* by the government? All this talk about humane treatment and minimizing property losses—you mean to tell me, you really believe them after what's happened to the people who own businesses in *Nihonmachi?* They'll be lucky if they get 10 cents on the dollar for their stock."

Tomi shifted in her seat and looked at Bill with annoyance. Why did he have to nitpick everything, she thought. Why couldn't he leave well enough alone and go along with everyone?

Jack glared at Bill and answered, "Even if that were true, what makes you think it would be any different if we resisted? Are you aware that there is a resolution in Congress—right now—to pass an amendment in the Constitution to take away our citizenship because our parents are Japanese? Think about it! Just how far do you think we'd get with that kind of mentality in Washington?"

Tomi wondered if Jack was making up the part about the resolution. *It couldn't be true,* she thought. It sounded too bizarre.

"It would never pass in Congress," Bill said emphatically.

"Nonetheless, that's the extent that the hatred of the Japanese Americans has accelerated to," said Jack. "Bill, the JACL will stand by its decision to cooperate with the government. We decided it's the only way to prove our loyalty and prevent bloodshed. We don't have any choice. We'll seek judicial justice later when the time is right."

"Wait a second," said Alice. "Bill is right about the FBI and the Justice Department report. That should be enough to vindicate the *nisei.*"

"When are you two going to get it through your heads we don't have the political leverage to make any difference?" yelled Jack, pounding the table. "The Army has been allowed to deliberately disregard those reports and is hell-bent on moving us out, with the blessing of the President."

"Yeah, it's an election year and he needs the vote," said Tosh sarcastically.

Tomi noticed that George and Mack were starting to look alarmed. Like Tomi, they had felt some sort of intervention would occur. Now, they knew that was out of the question.

Tomi glanced up nervously at the large clock hanging on the wall behind Jack that read 7:30. Jack turned to follow her eyes and said, "You people better leave now or you're going to be caught in the curfew."

The room was filled with the sound of the chairs scraping on the wooden floor. Everyone filed out of the small room with Jack and Tosh bringing up the rear.

"Tosh and I still have a lot to do. Don't worry about us. The police know we are working with the Army and will give us an escort home," said Jack in a weary voice. He turned to Bill and extended his hand. "Well, Bill, we're really doing the same thing but using different approaches. I think what you're doing is gutsy but ill-timed. I'm sure you're aware of the ramifications of your actions. I can only wish you good luck."

Tomi watched Bill shake Jack's hand. "There's no backing out for me now," he said. "I know what I'm doing is right. I don't have a choice either. Good luck to both of you." He offered his outstretched hand to Tosh.

Jack and Tosh turned and walked back into the room. The furious clicking of the typewriter began again.

# 10

## "E-Day"

Today was Evacuation Day. Tomi awoke to the smell of toasted bread that had drifted up to her bedroom. She could picture Kiku standing by the small gas stove in the kitchen, placing the bread on the four-sided metal toaster as the old aluminum coffee pot started to percolate. She faintly heard her mother move through the empty house and call from the bottom of the stairs.

"Tomiko! George! Get up! We still have much to do before the Army truck arrives." Kiku always used Tomiko when she was angry or upset. The *"ko"* at the end of her name indicated the feminine gender. But, in fact, Tomi hated her name. It sounded so Oriental and foreign. She wished she had an American-sounding name like George.

Tomi heard her brother stir and groan in the next room. Their aching bodies were no match for the unyielding floor. She turned over on her stomach and plopped face down on the pillow. As she slowly opened her eyes, she noticed balls of dust gently rolling across the floor and thought: *Just like my life. Going nowhere.*

Almost everything in the house—including the beds—had been

sold to a used furniture store in preparation for "E-Day." There was no time to reflect or think about anything else except to be ready to leave with whatever each of them could carry as instructed.

The Army truck had been scheduled to arrive at the house at 10:30 a.m. Tomi rolled over on the cold linoleum floor and shivered as the damp morning air settled over her. She and George had gone to sleep around 3:30 a.m. She vaguely wondered if her parents had slept at all. She missed the sound of the radio playing and resented having to turn it in to the authorities as contraband along with her father's binoculars.

"Everything has been packed so make sure you sleep with your underwear on," Kiku had instructed Tomi and George the night before. "And put on your Sunday best in the morning. You must not disgrace yourselves by dressing sloppy. Always be proud and dignified. Remember, you are of Japanese descent," she emphasized.

Tomi put on her glasses and glanced over at the small pile of her belongings. A worn suitcase was open and her Sunday dress, sweater and coat lay on top. She put on the dress and sweater and reached for her shoes and socks. Just as she finished putting on her shoes, Tomi heard Sam trot into the room. Sam was a stray mongrel that wandered into their yard many years ago when they lived crosstown on Ingersol Place. When they moved, they left him with their neighbors, the Kusudas. Weeks later Sam appeared on their back porch, dirty and thin with a look of indignation and reproach. Somehow he had tracked them down and reclaimed his place in the family. His calm and placid nature endeared him to everyone.

"Oh my gosh!" exclaimed Tomi. "We forgot all about you. What are we going to do?" She pounded on the wall of George's bedroom. "George, Sam is here! What shall I do?"

George rushed into Tomi's room and muttered, "Darn dog. What a time to show up!" He knelt down and nuzzled the dog and was rewarded with wet, affectionate licks. George sighed and said gruffly, "You're going to have to find a place for Sam. I have to help Papa clean up the house. Can't leave it dirty, you know. What about Mrs. Crabtree next door? She's not the best, but we don't have time to find anyone else."

"Not Mrs. Crabtree!" cried Tomi. "You know how she's always hollering at everyone. She's just like her name, crabby. Sam won't like her. Besides, how do I know she'll take him?"

"It's either that or the dog pound," George offered as he ran down the stairs.

Helen Crabtree was a middle-aged, Caucasian widow who had moved into the house next door two years ago. She kept to herself and seldom spoke to anyone. Her salt-and-pepper hair set off a stern face that never smiled. Once in a while she would appear on her front porch to yell at the children for making too much noise. Tomi felt Sam's future was bleak at best. She took him into the bathroom with her and the dog sat patiently as Tomi washed up and brushed her teeth. She reached down frequently to pet Sam and he responded with a low whine. He knows something is wrong, thought Tomi. "Wish you could go with me," she said to the dog. Sam softly thumped his tail and looked at her with gentle brown eyes. Tomi gathered her toiletries and wrapped them in a small towel. She hurried back into her bedroom with Sam trotting after her and threw the towel into the suitcase. Saburo appeared at the door.

"Tomi, finish your packing but leave the bedding. They have to be rolled tightly or they will unravel. Go help your mother clean up. The Army truck will be here soon." Saburo spoke rapidly as he moved into the room with a pair of large scissors and a bunch of rope hanging from his arm. He knelt on the floor to roll up the bedding.

After she closed her battered suitcase, Tomi flew down the stairs with Sam close at her heels. She peered into the living room to make sure her mother was not in sight. She saw a short rope hanging on the banister and tied it to Sam's collar.

"Come on, Sam," she whispered and yanked on the dog's collar as she led him out the front door. She saw Mrs. Crabtree sweeping her wooden front porch steps and approached her. The woman looked up and seemed to glare at Tomi and Sam.

"Yeah? What do you want?" she said rudely as she continued to sweep.

Tomi swallowed hard and said, "Mrs. Crabtree, could you take care of Sam until we come back? We have to go to a camp for a while…," her voice trailed off.

Finally Mrs. Crabtree looked up and asked sharply, "Why do you have to go to camp?" But her eyes softened as she looked at the young girl with the dog. Without waiting for an answer, she reached over and gruffly pulled Sam to her side.

Tomi could faintly hear her mother's irritated voice calling her name and she ran back toward the house as she gave a hasty "Thank you" to Mrs. Crabtree. She stopped at the edge of the lawn and glanced back. She could see Sam with his head held low and his legs rigidly planted in the grass, resisting Mrs. Crabtree's efforts to lead him away. His sharp, high-pitched cry followed Tomi as she rushed back to her house.

"I told you to hurry up! What are you doing outside, you foolish girl!" Kiku admonished her in Japanese. "Make sure you eat something and clean up the kitchen. Pack the coffee pot and toaster in that box," she continued and pointed to a small carton filled with kitchen utensils.

Kiku rushed out of the kitchen as George entered.

"Well, what about Sam?" he asked.

Tomi told him about Mrs. Crabtree's reluctant offer to take Sam and was rewarded with a big grin from George.

Saburo's voice cut through their moment of lightness.

"Oi! Everyone come here immediately!" he yelled. They rushed into the living room where he was standing with his hands on his hips.

Looking alarmed, Kiku asked, "What has happened?"

"Yamashita-san just came by and said that the Army truck will not be picking up our belongings. We will have to carry everything down the hill to the end of the block, and a bus will pick us up."

"Is that all?" said Kiku, feeling relieved. "I thought something terrible had happened."

"Well," said George, "at least we won't be shoved into those huge trucks with our luggage and look like a bunch of cattle like Steve and his family did in California." He was referring to the letter his cousin had mailed from the Santa Anita Assembly Center. "Do you know they even censored his mail?"

"Do not complain," said Kiku. "You must learn to *gaman*. You must learn to endure."

"What about Mack and his mother, Tomi?" George asked. "He hasn't been around lately."

"Last I heard, Mack was going to drive his mother to the Assembly Center. I don't even know which of the four camps he'll be in. He was upset because they told him his car would be impounded as soon as he got there. I guess he'll never see that car again," she sighed.

"Don't stand around and talk," scolded Saburo. "It is almost time to leave and the house is not cleaned up yet."

Finally a small pile of suitcases, three large duffel bags and assorted boxes stood neatly stacked in the middle of the living room. Each piece was tagged with a long, white cardboard imprinted with the family number, 17337. Saburo left a tag for each member of the family to wear for identification. The frantic pace escalated as everyone scurried to finish last minute chores and get dressed for the bus ride to the Puyallup Assembly Center, their next home.

The day was damp. It was starting to rain again and a coldness filled the empty house. Hurriedly, everyone changed their clothes. Saburo put on his navy suit, white shirt and tie. He struggled into a heavy overcoat and carefully placed his hat on his head.

Kiku put on her Sunday dress and a heavy beige sweater. She completed her outfit with a heavy brown topcoat and a dark brown felt hat. They looked as if they were going to a festive occasion.

"Where's your tie, George?" asked Tomi.

"In my jacket pocket. If I have to lug all this stuff around, I don't want to hang myself," he answered with a wry grin.

"Well, I'm wearing my Sunday dress and shoes. Gotta look good," Tomi said as she slipped into her winter coat. She tied on a babushka and picked up a family tag and let it dangle from the buttonhole of her coat.

Tomi stepped out the front door with her suitcase, dragging her duffel bag behind her. The small street was filled with people carrying suitcases, bedding and other paraphernalia down the hill. A low buzz spread through the crowd as the time to load the buses drew closer.

"*Hayaku, hayaku,*" Saburo urged. *Hurry.*

Just then, one of the duffel bags George had placed on the curb flopped over and started to roll slowly down the hill. George ran after the bag and found it wedged in the tall grass.

Out of the corner of her eyes Tomi spotted Mrs. Crabtree standing on her porch. She was crying. She kept dabbing her face with the front of her apron and shaking her head. Tomi was surprised at Mrs. Crabtree's unexpected reaction to their departure, but by now Tomi was feeling detached and uncaring about her surroundings. When she heard Sam howling from the backyard, she turned and walked down the hill without emotion to the waiting bus.

A young Caucasian soldier with a rifle slung over his shoulder stood nervously by the bus with a clipboard in his hand. He had on a heavy drab-olive overcoat over his uniform and towered over the crowd of people milling around the bus with their belongings.

Tomi noticed the jovial mood of the people. She heard laughter and joking as the crowd pressed toward the bus. Piles of suitcases and duffel bags began to accumulate. There was an air of anticipation. After all, the JACL had assured the Japanese community that the United States government had promised that the temporary camps were just a prelude to a semi-permanent camp where the conditions would be humane and comfortable—a haven of protective custody. Tomi also remembered hearing Congressman Hickle of Seattle speak on KOMO radio station:

> *The Japanese Americans can contribute to the war effort and show proof of their loyalty to the United States by cooperating with the military orders to be interned.*

Somehow, the statement did not ring true, but no one was questioning it by now, including Tomi.

# 11

## Camp Harmony

"Who named this place Camp Harmony anyway?" asked George. "It's a dump!" He was standing in the middle of a 20-square-foot room holding a straw-filled tick. "Better get over to the stall, Tomi, and fill your mattress cover or you'll have nothing to sleep on."

Tomi wasn't listening. Getting a straw mattress was not high on her agenda at that moment. She had gotten back from the ladies' room and was horrified to find a smelly latrine with six holes cut into two wooden planks laid back to back and no privacy. How was she going to change her sanitary napkins when she had her periods? How was she going to go to the bathroom with no privacy? Tomi surveyed her new home and saw four Army cots, a potbelly stove, and all the family belongings scattered in the small room. Two of the cots had lumpy mattresses on them.

"Tomi, go fill up your mattress," ordered Saburo.

"Did you see the bathroom, Papa? They're just holes in a board! The showers aren't much better either. There's no privacy at all! It's all open. I can't take a shower like that with everyone watching! I won't do it." Tomi's words tumbled out in English and Japanese.

Saburo looked at his daughter with a stern expression. Tomi cringed and waited for the recriminatory onslaught.

"Go," said Saburo, and Tomi ran out of the room into the muddy road in search of the straw. She sloshed through the mud until she heard voices. Tomi walked into a stable where a pile of straw lay on the ground. There was a small crowd of people filling their ticks. She quickly filled hers and started back to her barrack. Tomi heard someone call her name and saw a familiar figure running toward her. It was Mabel.

"Hey, slow down. You're splashing mud all over me," Tomi grumbled.

"Golly, not even a 'hello'?" teased Mabel. "I haven't seen you for weeks. Where's your room?"

"It's about four barracks down from here. Look, why don't you help me take this mattress back to my barrack, and I'll help you with yours."

"Okay by me," said Mabel cheerfully.

The two girls carried the mattress back to the barrack where Kiku and Saburo had given a semblance of order to the small room. Two cots were placed on one side of the room and two more were on the opposite side with a sheet hung in between. Mabel paid her respects to Tomi's parents, and the two girls returned to the stable where the straw was stored. After filling her mattress, Mabel led Tomi to an adjoining stable that was whitewashed and partitioned off. Mabel's mother, Yae, was sweeping the dirt into the cracks of the floor. She looked up as the girls entered the door and greeted them with a tired smile.

"We are fortunate to have this room," Yae said. "Those people with rooms under the grandstand have to leave the lights on day and night because there are no windows in there. It's pitch dark. At least we have a window."

Tomi helped Mabel make up her bed and left as soon as she could. She felt lucky to have a room in the barracks instead of the stables like Mabel, even if she had to share it with the whole family. Tomi hurried back and left her muddy shoes outside the door, only to step into a room full of sand.

There was a knock on the door, and Kiku went to answer it. "Who can *that* be. No one knows we are here—we only got here this morning."

Tomi, who was sitting on her bed behind the sheet, heard a male voice say, "I am Dave Higa, Interior Police. I would like to speak to the young lady who just walked in." He spoke perfect Japanese.

Tomi heard the alarm in her mother's voice as she asked, "What is wrong? What has she done?"

Tomi felt her heart start to beat rapidly and her hands became clammy. What do the police want with *me,* she wondered. She fearfully stepped forward from behind the sheet and saw a wiry but handsome young man with a roguish smile. His cap was slanted at a jaunty angle.

"Just want to warn you that you are not allowed to go into another area without permission," he said. "I saw you come out of Area B, and this is Area C. Here's a copy of the rules and regulations." He handed her a sheet of paper and touched the rim of his cap with a smile.

Just as soon as the policeman left, George walked in and asked, "What did he want?"

"Never mind," said Tomi, scanning the sheet. "You gotta hear this. It says there will be a door-to-door roll call twice a day, a curfew from 10 p.m. to 6 a.m., and lights off at 10:30 p.m. What do you think of that?"

"That's nothing. I just heard that the Interior Police can barge into the rooms anytime they want—without knocking."

Each of them was feeling dejected. Kiku sighed as she unpacked her duffel bag. Her main concern was to make the room livable. She wondered how to cover the window and keep the sand from getting in through the walls. She wished she had packed more fabrics so she could make curtains and dividers for the room. She glanced at the sandy floor and noticed sprigs of grass popping up through the wooden planks.

Saburo was unusually quiet. George eyed his father from across the room. In the last two weeks he had seen this tyrant turn into a meek conformist. He felt betrayed and angry with his father but could not sort out his feelings.

Tomi felt disgusted. It was clear to her the government was not keeping its promise. She was tired of hearing Kiku say, "It is your place to *gaman*." The thought of taking a shower with strangers made her shudder. Going to the latrine was even worse. And yet, she still held hope that conditions would get better.

After the initial wave of despair had subsided, the family members went to find the mess hall for their first meal in Camp Harmony. They picked their way through the mud and found the long line that snaked into the mess hall. The line inched forward slowly as a light drizzle fell on the crowd. Inside, Tomi could see people sitting at rows of long tables and benches eating canned wieners and boiled potatoes. She took one look at what was on the plates and walked out. Hungry as she was, the thought of eating canned wieners turned her stomach. Tomi found her way back to the barrack and rummaged through her belongings until she found a smashed peanut butter sandwich, which she promptly devoured. She was glad her mother had insisted they make sandwiches to bring with them.

Shortly after, George walked in and said, "Okay, where's the sandwiches? I know you brought them."

Tomi threw the bag to him and together they ate the rest as they sat on their cots.

"Better than the junk they have in the mess hall, huh?" she commented.

"Yeah. I don't see how Mama and Papa can eat that stuff."

"Wonder what we're eating tomorrow?"

"I wonder," George answered.

* * *

It was almost 10:30 p.m. when the day slowed to an uneasy halt. The anguish of the camp's occupants was intensified by the melancholic sound of the rain tapping against the tar paper roof on the barracks.

The Internal Police started to make their first round, and the opening and banging of the doors echoed through the barracks as they took roll. Saburo was trying to coax the wet wood in the potbelly stove to burn. He had found some scrap lumber and brought it back to the room. The light from a single bulb hanging from the middle of the ceiling made the room eerie.

Tomi could hear the murmur of people talking in the next room. She noticed there was an opening between the walls and the ceiling to accommodate a common flue with their neighbor's stove. Voices floated through the opening, and she found the intrusion disturbing. She undressed with her back to George and got into bed. The straw made the mattress feel lumpy and rustled at the slightest move. Tomi was exhausted, but unfamiliar sounds kept pulling her back to consciousness. She could hear a child's faint whimper, then the sound of a potty being used and its lid reverberating. Someone cleared their throat, and the sound of gentle snoring swelled to a snort and dropped to a sigh. Tomi finally fell into a fitful sleep.

The next morning, the insistent clanging of metal echoed across the barracks in Area C where Tomi and her family were assigned. Tomi was groggy with sleep and the traumatic events of the day before were still with her.

"What is that racket?" asked George irritably. "It's barely 6 o'clock." He flopped over on his cot without waiting for an answer and covered his head with a pillow.

Tomi could hear the people in the barrack stirring. The sound of muffled voices drifted into the small room where her family slept. Tomi found herself awakening and surrendering to the restrictive rules of Camp Harmony. She heard sloshing boots approach their barrack and stop at the door. There was a loud knock and a male voice penetrated the uncertainty of the morning.

"Morning! Roll call!" the voice announced. Tomi could see the doorknob turning and she pulled her blanket toward her face. The door opened slightly. She made out a male figure halfway in the room.

"It's me, Dave Higa, from the Internal Police Department. Remember? I talked to you people yesterday." Dave kept his head down and averted his eyes from the cots as he spoke. He proceeded to take roll and started to leave.

"What's all that clanging noise?" George asked without opening his eyes. His voice was heavy with sleep.

Dave chuckled. "You must be a city boy. That means chowtime on the farm," he said as he slammed the door and proceeded to the next family.

By now Tomi was wide awake and she could hear the rustle of clothing as Kiku and Saburo silently dressed behind the makeshift curtain. Her parents were not in the habit of greeting each other and the silence was intense. As usual, Saburo's surly mood dominated the family milieu.

As Tomi lay on her cot, she could feel a heaviness in her groin, and a slight cramp gnawed at her stomach. She knew her period had started. Gotta get to the bathroom fast, she thought. She dressed quickly and pulled out a sanitary napkin and a Kotex belt from her suitcase and shoved them inside her sweater. She dreaded going to the smelly latrine, but the sticky fluid chafing her thighs gave her no choice.

Tomi's attempt to hurry to the latrine was impeded by the mud that was pulling at her shoes, and each step was a struggle to move forward. The sky was dark and gray. The rain was drizzling and Tomi pulled her sweater close to her body to ward off the dampness. She squinted to look for the latrine and finally spotted it a couple of barracks away. She was hoping there would be no one using the latrine so that she could get her Kotex on without being observed. As she entered the wooden structure, Tomi was relieved to find it almost empty. An older *issei* woman brushed past her with her head down and eyes averted. Just as she reached into her sweater for the Kotex, Tomi heard a woman's loud voice and heavy footsteps leading into the latrine.

"Ugh! What a terrible smell," said the voice in Japanese. A short, fat woman entered and wobbled to a hole. She unceremoniously pulled down her underwear and defecated loudly. The woman looked up at Tomi who was standing dumbfounded by the next hole.

"Well, what are you standing there for? This is the women's toilet, you know. I see you have your period. You should take care of yourself. I have three girls I am raising myself. I hear they're going to ration toilet paper, and they just better give me a large ration. Do you realize how much toilet paper the girls need? What is your name?" The fat woman spoke as she wiped herself. Before Tomi could say a word, she continued. "I am Mrs. Oyama and I have three daughters…."

Tomi was mortified and embarrassed by Mrs. Oyama's directness and lack of finesse, and did not hear the rest of her prattle. Tomi quickly cleaned up and fled the building with Mrs. Oyama still chattering away. It was only when she neared her barrack that she realized she was so unnerved by Mrs. Oyama's coarse demeanor, she forgot to urinate. Tomi's indoctrination at the latrine was not complete. She let out a big sigh and went back toward the latrine again.

# 12

## Abandoned

It was exactly a month since Tomi had entered Camp Harmony. Miss Nellie Parker waited nervously in the small visitor's waiting room for her to arrive. Miss Parker sat primly on a hard wooden bench with her hands clasped tightly together and feet planted on the muddy wooden floor. She had placed her purse on top of the large package next to her. In it was a pair of boots, which she had bought at Penney's at Tomi's request. Behind her was a drafty window where she could see the rolls of barbed wire that framed the entrance to Camp Harmony. Two young soldiers strode back and forth at the entrance, and each visitor was scrutinized and checked before being granted entry. Beyond the barbed wire, Miss Parker could see the townspeople of Puyallup as they went about their daily routine.

She heard a commotion as children rushed to the barbed-wire fence to buy candy and snacks from local store owners who set up shop on the other side. The adults waited patiently for the children to finish their purchases so they could buy food to supplement the mess hall's meager diet. The armed soldiers ignored the transactions as they continued to guard the entrance.

Tomi entered the visitor's room and greeted her visitor. "Hello, Miss Parker. Thank you for coming and bringing my boots. I can really use them."

Miss Parker stood up and grasped Tomi's hand. "Are you all right?" she asked anxiously.

"Oh yes, Miss Parker. I'm fine," her voice trailed off into an awkward silence. Tomi knew that Nellie Parker, the church youth advisor, was feeling uncomfortable but did not know how to make her feel at ease.

"Do you need anything else?" asked Miss Parker. "A radio? Hot plate? Scissors?" her words tumbled out.

"Not really," said Tomi. "A couple of days ago, we were told to turn in all contraband, so I guess we won't be needing those things for a while."

"Oh!" Nellie was stunned.

"Um, how much for the boots?" asked Tomi.

"Nothing, nothing. Please. Allow me to get them for you."

A surge of anger welled up in Tomi's chest. She resented Miss Parker's show of pity but hid it with a tight smile and said, "Thank you but I have the money here." She held the money out to Miss Parker who took it reluctantly. The next half-hour was spent in an uncomfortable dialogue between the two women.

"I understand this camp is built on the Puyallup Fairgrounds and will accommodate 7,000 people," said Miss Parker trying to make small talk.

"Yes, it's hard to believe they built it in one month," answered Tomi. What she really wanted to tell her was how betrayed she felt by her own government and how she hated being locked up. Instead, she diverted Miss Parker's attention to another area across the street and pointed out the roller coaster.

"How strange to see the roller coaster area separated by barbed wire," said Miss Parker. "It looks out of place."

"It is out of place," Tomi murmured.

Miss Parker handed Tomi her boots. "God be with you," she said quietly and left.

Tomi cradled the box in her arms and started back to her barrack. As she sloshed her way through the mud, she felt her anger give way to guilt. She felt torn between her feelings of resentment and gratitude toward Miss Parker, who had driven 35 miles from Seattle to bring her the boots and whose only desire was to help her. Tomi saw a small pile of scrap lumber piled against a small shed and perched herself on top. She pulled out the boots and exchanged them for the wet, muddy saddle shoes she had on. She slid off the lumber pile and felt the soles of the boots sink into the mud.

"Hey, Tomi, is that you?" called a familiar voice. "Where did you get the new boots?" It was Mack.

Tomi had not seen or heard from him since she entered camp, and she was miffed at his lack of concern for her. "Where did *you* come from?" she asked as she struggled to pull herself out of the mud.

"Area A." Mack extended his hand to help her. "I'm sure glad I bumped into you. I really intended to look you up, but I've been busy working in the canteen. By the way, the FBI finally decided my father was not subversive and is letting him join my mother and me soon. I have to go to the Ad [Administration] building today and fill out some papers."

Tomi allowed Mack to help her out of the mud and told him about Nellie Parker's visit. Together they walked toward her barrack, making small talk. Tomi was aware that her feeling toward him had cooled since they last met, and she could feel an uneasy tension building a wall between them.

"So, when is your father going to come back here?" She asked politely.

"I got a hunch they're going to wait 'til we go to the permanent camp to move him."

"Well, maybe the FBI will take my father instead," Tomi snickered sarcastically.

Alarmed, Mack stopped short. "Why do you say that?"

"Well, it's really not funny, but my father blew his top at the Security Police last week. Remember when the administration sent notices for everyone to turn in all books written in Japanese?"

"Yeah?"

"Well, when the Internal Security Police showed up, my father got mad and screamed at them to get out. He told them he wasn't going to turn in his books, and they threatened to turn him in." Tomi looked anxiously at Mack and continued, "Do you think they'll really turn him in?" As much as Tomi abhorred Saburo's temper tantrums, it frightened her to think that her father would be taken away.

"Naw," said Mack, "I know those guys in Security. They would never do that. After all, they're all *nisei*. They had to say that. It's their job. They know those books are harmless, but some white bastard in administration got the idea of collecting and checking all reading materials."

"I hope you're right." Tomi drew a deep sigh of relief. She could hear the bitterness in Mack's voice, but it felt good to be able to confide in him. However, she was aware the rift between them had begun to widen and knew it was a matter of time before they would drift apart.

As Tomi and Mack entered the room, Kiku's eyes lit up and she greeted him warmly. She had always approved of Mack and was fond of him. Saburo, on the other hand, lay prone on his cot where he was reading his forbidden book. He looked up and glared over his glasses at Mack with a grunt. Kiku chattered on as Mack stood awkwardly in the middle of the small room not knowing where to sit. There were no chairs and he was not sure he should sit on any of the cots. Finally, he paid his respects to Kiku and Saburo and halfheartedly promised Tomi he would be in touch.

As the days passed, Tomi's life in Camp Harmony became tedious and mundane. She felt bored and depressed. The constant bombardment of petty rules and regulations was annoying. There were no classes to attend and her friends were scattered in four different areas of the camp. She roamed the camp but stayed away from the small cliques that started to form. One day, George announced that he had taken a job as a cook's help in the mess hall for $8 a month.

"Wow. How come so much money?" said Tomi sarcastically.

"Well, the government figures we get free room and board plus medical care so eight bucks should be enough," answered George with a wry smile. "That's nothing," he continued, "the professionals like Dr. Ogino get $16 a month."

"That should go over really big."

"Don't forget, we all get $2.50 a month for clothing allowance," he added.

"Yeah, and you can get those awful looking Army surplus clothes. They're all that yucky green color."

"They're not that bad." George held up a dark green vest. I think I'll go back and get a jacket too."

"Ugh," she muttered. "I wouldn't be caught dead in one of those things. I don't care how cold it is. Don't you know these things are from World War I?"

"What's the difference? You and your clothes."

"I know what Mama would say," said Tomi mischievously.

"*Gaman!*" they shouted in unison and laughed.

* * *

By end of April, the cold, damp spring weather had started to yield to the warmth of the approaching summer. Looking beyond the barbed-wire fence, Tomi could see the roller coaster silhouetted against the sky as if frozen in time. It had become a silent monument of what was once her outside world as it blended into the monotonous dreary weather. For the past few months, the rainy weather had covered the countryside with dull brown dirt and shrouded the sky with billowing gray clouds that wept ceaselessly.

Tomi marveled as she watched the breaking sunlight bathe the roller coaster. The sunbeam danced on the brightly painted metal as if to awaken the sleeping giant. Somehow, the arrival of summer raised her hopes for better days ahead. There were rumors of a move to a permanent camp. Surely the new camp would be more livable. As the days became warmer, the chasm of mud shrank into separate puddles and those eventually disappeared into dust and dirt. But the tar-papered roofs were no match for the summer sun, and Tomi spent many hours looking for a cool place to relax.

As Tomi predicted, Mack's visits became fewer, with long periods of absence in between. Saburo went over the edge on a rare day when Mack had come over and left. Saburo was lying on the cot with his hands behind his head. He watched Tomi with narrowed eyes and glared at her without saying anything. Finally, he said in Japanese, "I don't want you to go out with Mack anymore." Tomi was surprised and had nothing to say in response.

"He is too old for you, and you will do as I say," Saburo spoke in a cold, deliberate voice. He did not move from the cot.

Tomi stood in the middle of the room in stunned silence. She did not understand her father's attitude, since Mack had not been coming around recently. She was bewildered by his actions.

"Did you hear me?" he yelled and sat bolt upright on the cot. His sudden move made Tomi jump. She noticed the family in the next room had quieted down to listen as Saburo roared at her.

"Yes, Papa." Her voice quivered, and she ran out of the room to escape her father's rage. She found refuge in the laundry room and wanted to curl up into a ball and cry, but it was filled with women gathered around the sink, scrubbing their clothes and gossiping. Tomi found a small wooden bench in the corner and sat there trying to look nonchalant. She could feel her stomach churning as she struggled to maintain her composure. She closed her eyes for a moment when she heard a loud voice join the gossiping women. It was the woman she had encountered in the latrine on her first day at camp. She had no desire to deal with Mrs. Oyama and quickly exited from the other end of the laundry room. She wandered between the barracks until dinnertime.

Tomi got into the line when the familiar clanging announced dinnertime. As she neared the serving table she heard a murmur rumbling down the line.

"What *is* that thing?" someone asked.

"Just be quiet and eat it," ordered the cook.

When Tomi reached the serving counter, she was shaken to see several huge trays lined with rolls and rolls of boiled cow's tongue. The rigid, headless tongues seemed to be mocking her as they lay on the metal trays. Tomi looked at the dull, brownish meat with a tinge of color running through it and promptly lost her appetite.

The cook was slicing each one in huge chunks but almost everyone declined their share.

"Don't you know cow's tongue is considered a delicacy?" declared a middle-aged man. Everyone politely refused to comment.

"Learn to cook!" a bold diner shouted. An older *issei* gave the heckler a scathing look. It was not polite to point out anyone's glaring blunder. Nervous laughter trickled through the line. Tomi refused her portion of tongue but picked up a bowl of rice and a small dish of Japanese pickles. Although the food had improved since the first day, today was not one of them. There were days when fresh fruit and vegetables were served, and the children got their share of milk. But the chef's skill determined how well each block ate. Tomi regretted their misfortune of getting someone so unimaginative.

As she returned her tray and utensils, Tomi saw George standing behind the serving counter. He motioned her over and told her to wait for him.

"I'll be through in 10 minutes. I have to talk to you so wait in the back," he said in a solemn voice. He spoke loudly over the din of clattering dishes and pans.

"Guess you heard about Papa and me, huh," said Tomi.

"It's more than that—it's what happened *after* you left."

"Now what?" Tomi muttered as she waited for George to finish his duties.

By the time George was through cleaning the serving counter, the mess hall was almost empty. Two women remained to arrange the stacks of dishes, cups and utensils for the next meal. The huge empty room echoed with the sound of clattering dishes. George joined Tomi in the back of the mess hall where she was waiting.

"I already know what happened between you and Papa," George said. "When I got home this afternoon, he was still ranting and raving about you and Mack. Finally, I told him to leave you alone and—"

"You did?" asked Tomi incredulously. George rarely intervened on her behalf.

"Yeah, and before I knew it, he came after me so I raised my arm to stop him. I thought he was going to hit me," said George. "All of a sudden he started to accuse me of trying to strike him. Then he turned to Mama and yelled at her, saying he could never live with a son who would strike his own father for any reason and that he was leaving. He was yelling so loud the whole barrack heard him!"

"How embarrassing," said Tomi.

"Boy, I don't know what got into him," continued George. "Then Papa threw his things into a duffel bag and left. I don't know where he went, but he's gone." George shrugged in dismay.

Tomi was relieved. Now, she could go back to the barrack without fear of her father's rage. She knew he couldn't go too far within the confines of the barbed wire. "What did Mama say?"

"She says Papa is using the fight between me and him as an excuse to leave, and I think she's right."

"So do I," she said, nodding her head. "What he said doesn't make sense."

They returned to their barrack where they found Kiku sitting on her cot mending clothes. She looked up briefly from her work and said, "Your father is no longer living here. The block manager came by to tell me his cot will be picked up tomorrow and that your father will be living in the bachelor's quarters." Her voice was matter of fact and indifferent. The rest of the evening was spent breaking down Saburo's cot and rearranging the room.

# 13

## Journey to "the Garden of Eden"

The arrival of summer not only brought Camp Harmony relief from the rain, but also seemed to ease the wrath of the Wartime Civil Control Administration, which relaxed its restrictions on contraband, reading materials and activities.

Nellie Parker visited whenever she could and brought the small Zenith radio and portable typewriter that Tomi had left in her care. Tomi placed them on a small shelf that George had put together with scraps of green lumber. She envied her neighbors, who were able to find tools to make chairs and tables for their room. Kiku found a large wooden box, and together they laid a wide plank on top to make a table. Tomi helped her mother cover the window with an old towel to cut the glare of the searchlight that swept the barracks all night.

Six months after they had arrived at Camp Harmony, the evacuees were given orders to move. The news was welcomed by Tomi. She had been hearing about the new camp since their neighbor, Mr. Kitahara, announced he was going to Minidoka, Idaho, to help get it ready for the people temporarily housed in Camp Harmony.

That was a month ago. To her, this new camp meant a more stable lifestyle. Rumors trickled back to the people about the negative aspects of their future home, but Tomi refused to listen. Surely the government would keep their word to provide comfortable living quarters.

\* \* \*

Finally the day arrived to board the train headed to their final destination. The soldiers cordoned off a path to herd the people onto the train. It was an orderly crowd, with many of the men assisting the soldiers in loading the people and baggage. Tomi and Kiku boarded and found two seats facing each other. Tomi took a window seat and George sat next to her. They saw a long line of soldiers in combat gear facing the train, all with rifles at their sides. Their presence was ominous. After what seemed like a long time, the train started to pull away. A soldier with a rifle slung over his shoulder kept pace with the slow-moving train and motioned Tomi to close the blinds. The loud clanging bells and hissing engine drowned out his voice, and the last thing she saw was his boots as she complied.

The train coughed and jerked and slowly picked up speed. The wheels creaked until the train finally settled into a rhythmic rocking motion. Tomi sat up straight in the hard, unyielding seat across from her mother and tried to get comfortable. As their eyes met, Kiku leaned toward her and whispered, *"Shikkari, ne."* *Be strong.*

The train's movement lulled her into a deep trance. It was the middle of August, and the train pushed forward in the summer heat. The low buzzing of people talking filtered in and out of her consciousness, but she dared not give in to sleep and disgrace herself. She had to be in control of herself at all times.

Once in a while Tomi could hear a mother comforting a crying baby. Most of the children sat quietly in their seats under the watchful eyes of their parents. They were intrigued by the MP who strolled up and down the aisles. She could feel the tension of the people beginning to mount as the heat became unbearable, and a wave of uneasiness swept over them.

Twenty-seven hours later, the train pulled into the Jerome, Idaho, station where the ritual of unloading and loading was repeated. Tomi climbed into an Army truck with Kiku and George, and soon they were part of a convoy. The huge wheels on the trucks stirred up the dry dirt, and the vehicles became a gigantic caterpillar inching its way across the Idaho plain. There was no way to escape the onslaught of dust in their hair, eyes and mouths.

Tomi looked over at George and laughed at his appearance. "You sure look weird."

"You should look at yourself," he shot back.

When the trucks rolled to a stop, Tomi noticed that there was no barbed wire in sight. But before she could assess her new surroundings any further, she and the others were hustled into line to be registered, fingerprinted and examined by a doctor. Finally, they were assigned their apartments.

It was not until the maintenance truck dropped them off at their new barrack that Tomi was able to take full stock of her surroundings. What she saw struck her with such force that she almost fell backward. Tomi was devastated—Minidoka was a replica of Camp Harmony that stretched leisurely across the Idaho reclamation land. She noticed many of the buildings were not completed. The only difference was that the barracks in Minidoka were built above the ground with three steps leading up to the rooms. Everything else was a duplicate of the latrines, showers, laundry rooms and mess hall they had just left in Camp Harmony. Nothing had changed except for the vast corridor of dust bowl they nicknamed "The Garden of Eden." This was now their home.

Tomi felt lightheaded and her knees started to buckle. Her hands flew to her mouth, but it was too late. She heard herself screaming, "Oh my God!"

George turned toward her. He shrugged, gave a sigh and raised both arms in the air helplessly.

Kiku marched up the steps to the apartment and glared at her daughter.

"Get in here," she ordered in an icy tone. "Have you no shame? What will people think of you?" She jerked the door open and entered without looking back. Kiku was embarrassed that her young daughter could not control her emotions.

Tomi felt drained and betrayed. She didn't care what her mother thought. All she could think was that they had been deceived again.

"Come on, Tomi. Let's go in," George said gruffly.

They entered their new "apartment." The address above the door read, Block 21, Barrack 5A.

\* \* \*

It started with a small whirl of sand circling her ankles. Tomi noticed small waves of sand starting to shift gently across the plain. Looks like a sandstorm coming up, she thought, and put it out of her mind. Tomi was walking back from the canteen where she had purchased a toothbrush. As the whirling sand started to gain momentum, she quickened her pace but wasn't worried. She only had one more block to go. There was plenty of time to get back home before the sandstorm started.

Suddenly the wind whipped the sand into a frenzy of motion. Tomi strained against the wind to move forward, and she could no longer see the outline of the surrounding barracks. The wind whirled around her wildly and jerked at her body and clothes. Her face was peppered with sand, and she could barely see where she was. She finally lost her sense of direction and no longer knew which way to go. As she struggled forward, Tomi saw the faint outline of a pole and managed to grab onto it. The onslaught of the wind and sand intensified and the loud whistling sound of the sandstorm frightened her. It was coming at her from all directions. For one wild moment she panicked. Her heart was beating very fast. She huddled against the pole and held on tight. Suddenly she felt a pair of strong arms wrap around her waist and heard someone yelling her name. She couldn't see who it was until her rescuer led her to the nearest barrack and helped her into a room.

"Ah, *Chibi-chan*," said Mr. Watanabe, using the term "little one" in Japanese. "What are you doing out in that sandstorm?"

Ichiro Watanabe was a widower. His daughter, Michiko, and Tomi had been childhood chums since grade school. He always called her *Chibi* because he thought she was so tiny. Tomi stood self-consciously in the middle of the room, trying not to spit out the sand that had crept into her mouth. She was embarrassed to have been rescued. Tomi was glad Michiko was not home. She would have teased Tomi mercilessly for getting caught in the sandstorm.

"Oh, Mr. Watanabe, I didn't know it was you. I couldn't see anything," said Tomi. "Thank you for helping me."

"I just happened to look out the window and thought you were a little dog," he teased. His pleasant round face broke out in a smile. "You should be more careful, Tomi. You could have been blown away."

"There are no dogs in the camp, Mr. Watanabe," said Tomi solemnly.

"I am only teasing you, *Chibi-chan,*" he replied as he slapped his knees and roared with laughter.

Tomi usually enjoyed his good humor and cheerful attitude, but the sandstorm had shaken her and she was anxious to get back to her own room.

The wind was beginning to abate, but with every surge of the wind, sand would blow through the cracks in the wall, and the floor was covered with the fine grains.

"Ah, I must fix those boards," said Mr. Watanabe. "They are

green and do not fit together well. If you wait awhile, Michiko will be back soon. She is with her auntie."

"Thank you, Mr. Watanabe, but I must get back. Tell Michi I'll see her later," said Tomi. She peered out the window and could see the surrounding barracks again.

Tomi paid her respects to Mr. Watanabe and returned to her barrack. Kiku and George were both waiting for her as she entered the room.

"We were worried about you. Don't you know better than to be out in that storm?" Kiku scolded.

"Nothing happened. I can take care of myself," she snapped.

Kiku stared at her sullen daughter and chose not to pursue the issue.

Tomi sat down on her cot and tried to shake the sand out of her hair.

George flopped down beside her. "Take it easy, Tomi. This isn't easy on anyone. Look, I hear they just opened up the hospital and they're really short on help. You want to go and sign up for work? It's better than sitting around all day and fighting with Mama."

George's news piqued Tomi's interest. She was tired of roaming the barracks all day with nothing to do. A job at the hospital might be interesting.

"Yeah, I wanna go. Maybe I can be a nurse's aide," she said excitedly. "They wear pink- and white-striped dirndl skirts with a bib and white blouse. It's really cute. I'll ask Michi if she wants to go too."

"You think I could fit into one of those dirndl skirts too?" asked George.

"What a nut!" said Tomi. "Let's go and apply right now."

# 14

## Angel of Mercy

"What do you mean you're both working in the tuberculosis ward?" asked Kiku. "Do you realize how contagious TB is?"

"They don't have enough help, Mama, and a lot of the nurses are afraid to work in that ward," answered Tomi.

"None of the kitchen help will work in the TB ward for the same reason, which means someone has to run the dishwasher and serve the food," explained George.

"So we decided to take the job," finished Tomi.

Kiku was incredulous at her children's lack of fear and common sense. "But they have professional doctors and nurses to run that ward. Why would you two deliberately expose yourselves to that dreaded disease? I don't understand," she said, waving her hands in exasperation.

"No, you don't understand, Mama. Right now, these people don't have anyone to take care of them," said Tomi. "George has the night shift, and Michi and I have the day shift."

"Do you mean to tell me Mr. Watanabe approves of Michiko working there?" Kiku asked.

"Not really. But he's leaving it up to her to decide."

"I certainly do not approve, but if you two insist on working there, make sure you do a good job," said Kiku. She turned away and busied herself with her sewing.

The hospital was built near the Administration building and away from the rest of the camp. Two rows of buildings were built parallel to each other and consisted of 15 wards. They were connected on both sides by a long hallway, which extended from the clinic on one end to the isolation ward on the other.

In spite of their mother's warning, Tomi and George spent the summer caring for the TB patients with very little supervision and help. The work was not physically demanding because most of the patients were ambulatory. Tomi learned to dispense medicine with the help of the patients who carefully watched the bottles with their names on it. The medications were labeled and sorted for each patient.

"Not the small pink one, Tomi," a patient would tell her, "the big pink one." Tomi had no idea what she was dispensing or why, but none of the patients complained. They were grateful for any help. George also dispensed medication and learned to use the automatic dishwasher. Men and women had separate rooms in the ward, which also had a special section for a group of younger men. Tomi and Michi enjoyed bantering with the seven young men who were well behaved but prone to gentle teasing and flirting with the two nurse's aides.

"Hey, good lookin'," Tom Hasegawa would say. "Can I have a date when I get out of here?"

"Only if you take your medicine," Tomi would come back.

If any of the men started to get too rowdy, Tom would bring them up short. "Hey, lay off. These girls are teenagers. Watch it," he would warn.

Tomi noticed one frail young man who sat on his bed and quietly read his book. Sometimes he would sit and watch the others play cards but kept to himself most of the time. Tomi looked up his chart and found that Tim Morita was only 19 years old. He probably feels out of place among the older guys, thought Tomi. He was so quiet, she and Michi sometimes forgot he was in the ward. Tim never complained about anything. It was nothing unusual for him to sleep his time away.

It was his mother, Chiyoko Morita, who noticed that her son was not feeling well. "I am sorry to bother you when you are so busy, but my son is complaining of a bad headache and he says he feels nauseous. Could you have a doctor look at him, please?" she pleaded.

"Oh, it's probably nothing, Mrs. Morita, but I will make a note on his chart for a doctor to look at him," said Tomi.

Chiyoko visited her son daily, and the following day, her request for a doctor became more insistent. "My son, Tim, is not doing well at all. Did you notice he still has a high fever?" she said. "Could you please make sure one of the doctors looks at him?"

Tomi looked at the small woman standing in front of her. Mrs. Morita was not one to make demands. "What's bothering Tim, Mrs. Morita? I put in a request for a doctor for you yesterday—no one came?" asked Tomi. She was getting alarmed. "Let's go take a look."

"I don't think he is conscious," said Chiyoko quietly as they walked into the men's ward.

Four of the men were playing cards and the other two were on their bed reading. They acknowledged her with a silent nod and continued their activities.

"Hey, is there something wrong with Tim?" asked Jake Wada. "He sure has been quiet the last couple of days."

"I don't know," answered Tomi. But as soon as she looked as Tim, she froze in her tracks. Tim was barely conscious. His eyes were closed and his mouth was slightly open. She could hear him moaning softly and he did not respond when she called his name.

Tomi went to the phone immediately and relayed Tim's condition to the head nurse.

Within minutes, the TB ward became a beehive of activity. Doctors and nurses dressed in masks and gowns burst into the ward. Tom and the others were moved into another room. By the time Tomi went off her shift, she saw Tim's room cordoned off except for the doctors and nurses rushing in and out. Once when the door opened, Tomi peered in and saw Tim's mother sitting quietly by his bed with her hands folded in her lap. Her face was expressionless as she watched the parade of people working over the fragile, limp body of her son.

Tomi tossed and turned that night and could not fall asleep. She heard George come in about 12:30 in the morning from his shift. "Pssst, George. How is Tim?" she asked in a whisper.

"Not good," said George. "They don't expect him to live. The doctors diagnosed his illness as spinal meningitis." George undressed in the dark and slid into his cot.

"What's that? Is it contagious?"

"Yep. It's some sort of infection of the nervous system. When you report for work tomorrow, you're going to get a gamma globulin shot. It's supposed to keep you from catching that disease. I already got one tonight from Dr. Ozawa."

Kiku shushed them. "Be quiet, both of you. You know the whole barrack can hear you. Be more considerate of other people."

"Ah, the hell with it!" snapped George. He was in no mood to follow his mother's code of conduct.

*"Joo-jii!"* hissed his mother. She always stretched out his name when she was angry with him.

"Okay, okay!"

\* \* \*

The next morning Tomi explained to her mother what had happened at the hospital. Kiku shook her head in sympathy.

Losing a child was one torment she understood. Kiku had never stopped grieving for the son she lost 15 years ago when he died of flu at the age of 4.

When Tomi arrived at work, the normal routine had not settled back in. She could feel the tension of the people working in the ward. The patients were quiet and pensive. The men who were moved out of Tim's ward were subdued and anxiously waiting for news of Tim's progress. Everyone, including the nurse's aides, was given the gamma globulin shots to protect them from the virus. Although no one verbalized their fears, Tomi was aware that everyone in the TB ward was worried about contracting spinal meningitis.

Tim's condition deteriorated rapidly. Despite the medical staff's efforts, he was not responding. By the end of the day his frail body had succumbed to the disease. Tim died in his mother's arms.

Tim's passing was devastating to Tomi and Michi. It was their first experience with the death of someone they had taken care of and knew by name. Somehow, they felt responsible. Tomi agonized over whether she should have called the doctor sooner. It was a burden she was to carry with her for many years.

The door to Tim's room opened, and Tomi saw his family file slowly out. Chiyoko Morita, her husband and younger son had paid their last respects. The hallway was bustling with people as the staff and patients milled around at the news of Tim's death.

Chiyoko spoke briefly to her husband and then walked toward the two girls. Tomi's heart leapt to her throat. She could feel the thump of her heart against her rib cage.

She's going to blame me for Tim's death, thought Tomi.

Chiyoko stopped directly in front of the two girls and bowed very low several times in the formal, traditional Japanese custom. The hallway suddenly became very quiet as all eyes turned to the grieving mother. Tomi could feel the blood rush to her head.

As Chiyoko spoke in formal Japanese, she stood very straight with her hands folded in front of her. Looking directly at each girl, she said, "On behalf of the Morita family, I would like to express my gratitude to both of you for taking care of our son, Tim. I cannot express how much we appreciate your kindness and dedication. We will never forget your compassion. Our most sincere thanks to both of you."

She bowed again and turned to join her family. No one spoke as the bereaved family silently left the ward. Tomi realized she had just watched a woman accept the death of her son with stoic calm in the most traditional manner. Chiyoko's eyes reflected great strength and dignity as she expressed her thanks. Tomi and Michi were overwhelmed by what they had just experienced, but neither girl shed a tear for Tim. It was as if they had invaded Chiyoko's solitude, and her grief was far beyond their comprehension. Tomi pushed her own feelings of grief deep within herself.

After Tim's death, more nurses were on hand and doctors started making regular rounds. A few weeks later, Tomi and Michi transferred to the general ward while George chose to remain in the TB ward.

Tomi always tried to avoid Dr. Ozawa. He was very demanding and expected the nurse's aides to behave and perform like professional nurses. He was a short man with an equally short temper. His voice was not loud but his constant ranting was a source of irritation to the staff as well as the patients. On one occasion, he caught Tomi attending a woman who had delivered a baby. He bombarded her with questions about the woman's condition.

"What are her medications? Date of delivery? Any temperature?" he asked.

"I don't know," Tomi answered repeatedly.

Dr. Ozawa's ranting turned into rage and his voice cracked. "You don't know? Your incompetence should not be tolerated!"

"But I'm only a nurse's aide," said Tomi meekly.

"It doesn't matter. I expect you to be able to perform in a professional manner!" he thundered.

Tomi was mortified. As soon as she could escape from Dr. Ozawa, she ran into the supply room and cowered in the corner where Yuki Suzuki, the head nurse, found her. Yuki was a woman in her early 30s who had been a nurse at the King County Hospital in Seattle. Nothing seemed to faze her calm demeanor. Tomi admired the cool detachment she displayed in times of crisis and the loving tenderness she showered on her patients.

"Well, what are you doing on the floor, Tomi?" Yuki leaned forward and offered her hands. "Are you sitting on a bedpan?" She laughed as she helped Tomi off the floor.

"Dr. Ozawa yelled at me for nothing. I hate him."

"Oh, don't mind him. He has a lot on his mind, Tomi. He just likes to yell. You know what? At 2 o'clock this afternoon I want you to take this patient down to the clinic at the end of the corridor for X-rays." She handed Tomi a slip of paper that read, *Taro Shoji, Bed 4A, Ward 7.* "Could you do that for me? You'll have to take him in a wheelchair, okay?"

"Sure, Miss Suzuki, I'll do it for you," promised Tomi.

At 2 o'clock, Tomi went to Ward 7, and Michi helped her put Taro Shoji into the wheelchair. He was an elderly man with a broken leg and looked undernourished and feeble. Michi placed the cast leg on the straight board extending from the wheelchair and placed a small lap blanket over his knees.

"There you are, Mr. Shoji. Are you comfortable?" she asked.

"*Arigato, arigato,*" said Taro, bowing his head several times to Michi.

"Okay," said Tomi. "See you later."

Tomi pushed Mr. Shoji out of the ward into the long corridor leading to the clinic. The heavy wheelchair was a relic from World War I. She could not see over the top of the chair but she noticed that it moved forward smoothly without any effort on her part. She could hear Mr. Shoji's soft voice speaking to her, but she did not catch the words. She appeased him by occasionally saying, "Uh huh. That's right, Mr. Shoji."

After a few minutes, Tomi noticed that the corridor was built on a slight incline and the momentum of the heavy wheelchair was picking up speed. She groped for the brakes on the side of the chair and could not reach them, so she tried to pull back on the chair, which was already out of control. She bent her knees and dragged her feet, but the wheelchair continued to hurtle down the corridor, pulling her along. She glanced around the side and saw the walls of the clinic rapidly approaching. She knew she had to do something quickly or Mr. Shoji would have another broken leg.

Just before the impact, Tomi braced herself and yanked the wheelchair to one side with all her strength. She sent it reeling on its two right wheels, slamming Mr. Shoji and the wheelchair against the wall. The momentum sent Tomi flying, and she crashed through a half-open door and landed face down inside an office. She raised her head and two pairs of shoes appeared at her eye level. She knew instinctively the shiny black pair belonged to Dr. Ozawa. He was the only doctor who wore that ugly style. Then she heard a familiar voice. She looked up and saw Nurse Suzuki.

"Oh dear!" she said, "What in the world happened? Are you all right, Tomi?"

Tomi quickly picked herself off the floor. She could see that Dr. Ozawa was livid. He was speechless, and his face was red with anger. Unable to speak, he shook his fingers at Tomi. Without answering Yuki, she hastily retreated to the clinic where a crowd of nurses were untangling Taro and calming the frantic man. Fortunately, he was not hurt, just badly shaken. He saw Tomi and flinched. He glared at her for good reason.

"*Da-me, da-me*," he said. *No good, no good*. He shook his head as an attendant wheeled him into the X-ray room.

Tomi returned to Ward 7 and explained to Michi what had happened. Michi was sympathetic and together they giggled at

Tomi's misfortune.

"Poor Mr. Shoji!" exclaimed Michi.

"Poor Mr. Shoji nothing," said Tomi. "What about me? Dr. Ozawa will probably yell at me again."

Just at that moment, Nurse Kamai walked by and motioned for Tomi to follow her. Without a word she led Tomi to the supply room of the men's surgical ward and handed her a urinal.

"I want you to take this urinal to Mr. Koto in bed 14A and take care of him," said Nurse Kamai briskly.

"Yes, Miss Kamai," she said. Mr. Koto was an elderly man who had his left leg amputated from the knee down. Tomi handed him the urinal and when he had finished, she disposed of the contents in the men's bathroom. Nurse Kamai appeared at the bathroom door.

"Did you wash your hands thoroughly? Mr. Koto has syphilis, you know," she said casually. "No one wants to take care of him."

Tomi's first reaction was shock followed by anger. It was all she could do to lash out at Nurse Kamai. She wanted to scream an obscenity at her. Instead she held herself in check and asked, "Why didn't you tell me he had syphilis?"

"Does it matter?" answered Nurse Kamai. "You're here to help." She glared at Tomi and walked away.

Michi walked in on Tomi as she stood at the sink, furiously scrubbing her hands.

"Gads, you look mad, Tomi. What's wrong?"

"Nothing! I'm quitting this lousy hospital. Stay if you want to, but I'm going!" Tomi turned on her heels and stomped out of the ward. Michi stood dumbfounded.

Tomi made her way down the dirt road leading from the hospital to the main road. Her eyes filled with hot tears, but she refused to give in. She burrowed both hands in the pocket of her apron and prepared for the long walk back to her barrack. She faintly heard someone calling her. It was Michi, who came running after her.

"Now what happened?" demanded Michi.

Tomi poured out her frustration about her latest encounter with Nurse Kamai. Michi listened quietly and occasionally murmured her sympathy. The girls looped their arms around each other's shoulders and started down the wide dirt road. They heard the rumbling of a vehicle behind them and moved to the right, just as a truck filled with a hooting maintenance crew sped past.

"Creeps!" Michi yelled as the cloud of dust and dirt covered the two girls. They walked in silence for a few minutes. Tomi looked over at Michi and started to giggle. Soon, they were both laughing so hard they had to let go of each other. When they reached the bottom of the hill, they collapsed in a heap. An old *issei* man walking by shook his head and muttered, "These *nisei* are so carefree...." He was not aware that laughter was their only alternative to tears.

# 15

## School Days

Minidoka was dubbed "The Garden of Eden" but did not live up to its name by any stretch of the imagination. The mosquitoes were another nuisance, attacking the evacuees with the precision of dive-bombers. The summer heat steadily increased and beat relentlessly on the thin roofs as the temperature crept above 100 degrees. The sandstorms were a routine occurrence and drove the women to distraction as they tried to keep the rooms clean.

Self-government, similar to the one in Camp Harmony, was set up with the blessings of the War Relocation Authority to restore a sense of normalcy. Soon an active community flourished within the confines of the barbed wire, and many of the Japanese cultural activities and classes were restored under the watchful eyes of the administration. None of these benefits interested Tomi, who continued to suppress her resentment.

Nellie Parker kept in touch with Tomi, and in one of her letters she explained that the Seattle Council of Churches was working to establish schools in the camp, which was not a major concern of the Army or the Wartime Civilian Control Administration.

*As you know, the Council of Churches worked hard to establish a vacation Bible school in Camp Harmony when it first opened but was turned down by the authorities and had to be abandoned until later. At that time we learned that no provision had been made for education or recreation for the people in the camps. The Council of Churches joined forces with the public schools to raise money and collect books to start a library in camp, which was successfully completed.*

*We do all this in fervent hopes for you and your friends to continue your education. We shall continue to work toward educational programs and hope to establish a certified school as soon as possible.*

Miss Parker went on to inform Tomi that a scholarship to Brown University would be available to her through the American Friends Committee as soon as she finished high school in camp. After she read the letter, Tomi decided she would not return to school. She was ashamed to tell Miss Parker that her grade point average would never warrant a scholarship. She felt trapped and resented Miss Parker's assumption she would accept the scholarship. The letter sent Tomi into abysses of despair. For days she moped around and snapped at George until he finally told her, "Cut it out! I don't know what's bothering you, but get off my back!"

Tomi fled to the laundry room to escape George's ire. She noticed a girl about her age curled up in her usual corner reading a magazine and noted with a tinge of derision that it was not proper for a girl to sit in public with her legs folded up. The girl looked up and greeted Tomi as she approached.

"Hi, you live in the barrack in front of me, right?"

"I don't know. I'm in 5A," replied Tomi.

"See? I'm in 4A. Why don't you sit down?" Tomi was taken aback by the girl's friendliness because it usually took several encounters before friendships developed. They introduced themselves, and Tomi was immediately drawn to Hana Yasui's natural charm. Her large-boned frame was a glaring contrast to Tomi's slight build. She had a light complexion and pink cheeks. Her smile lit up her face, and her eyes danced. It was what Tomi needed to draw herself out of the depths of self-pity.

Hana poked Tomi in the ribs and said, "Want to hear something funny?

Tomi grinned at her new friend and answered, "Okay, what?"

"Do you know what *min-na* means in Japanese?"

"It means 'everyone,'" answered Tomi.

"And *do-ka* is a slang word for 'how's things,' right?" Hana said, giggling. "Sooo, Minidoka means 'How-is-everyone' camp!"

"How corny!" moaned Tomi in mock horror, giggling.

Just then, Hana reached over and flipped on a small radio that was by her side. The soothing voice of Bing Crosby started to croon the song, "Don't Fence Me In," which sent both of them into another round of hysteria. Together they joined in, drowning out the music as they finished the song:

*And I can't look at hobbles*
*and I can't stand fences*
**Don't fence me in!**

Their peals of laughter echoed through the laundry room. Several *issei* women scrubbing clothes looked up and clucked their tongues in disapproval as they shook their heads and muttered, *"Nisei!"*

* * *

As summer released its fiery grip on Minidoka, fall arrived unnoticed. By now, five miles of barbed wire enclosed the self-contained community and eight watchtowers stood at attention like wooden sentries with machine guns pointed toward the camp. Autumn gave way to winter in all its majestic glory and held the camp in its grasp with icy fingers and sub-zero weather. Tomi swallowed her pride long enough to get a heavy Army jacket and leggings from the canteen to keep warm. After all, she reasoned, it was better to be warm than fashionable. The fallen snow softened the starkness of the barracks, and young trees planted in the spring were bejeweled with ice crystals that sparkled like precious stones. All too soon the weight of the heavy trucks and daily activities of the camp trampled the snow into slush and mud. Once again, Minidoka donned its dreary winter garb.

It was not long after the first snowfall when a hastily organized school got underway. Tomi braced herself to carry out her plans not to finish high school. She confided in Hana, who listened sympathetically and did not try to dissuade her.

"Okay, if that's what you really want," Hana said casually. "By the way, I have to talk to my core teacher tomorrow. Why don't you come with me?"

"Why?" asked Tomi suspiciously.

"Well, I thought we could go see the movie, 'The Son of Monte Cristo,' at the recreation hall afterward."

"Guess so."

Hana and Tomi entered the small classroom where Ethel Miller was rummaging through a pile of used textbooks. They saw a tall, Caucasian woman with light brown hair that was styled in a pompadour. A pair of narrow, rimless reading glasses set off blue-green eyes that darted to the girls as they approached. Mrs. Miller greeted the girls with a broad smile and asked warmly, "Well, who do we have here?" She continued to pull books out of the box as she peered over her glasses to read the titles. The two girls stood by shyly as Mrs. Miller pushed aside a pile of letters and papers and invited them to sit down.

"Now, which one of you is Hana Yasui?" she asked as she looked at a clipboard with a long list of names. Mrs. Miller proceeded to explain the curriculum to Hana and when she finished she turned to Tomi. "Who is your core teacher, dear?"

"No—no one," Tomi stammered. She was caught off guard. "I'm not signed up yet," she mumbled. "I'm leaving camp as soon as I can get a release."

"Sounds exciting, but what about high school? It would be difficult to attend school outside camp if you're working, wouldn't it?" she asked gently.

Tomi's words tumbled out in a torrent of rage. "What's the difference? I have no future. The only job I can get now is as a house girl. You don't need an education for that! All I want to do is to get out of this stupid camp. I can't stand being locked up like this. I want to be out! Free! I don't care about school." As soon as she finished, Tomi was mortified. She had committed the cardinal sin of talking back to a teacher. Hana looked embarrassed as both girls anticipated a tongue-lashing from Mrs. Miller.

Instead, she leaned over to Tomi and said, "I understand your feelings, but as a teacher, I have to tell you that finishing school will be in your best interest. No one will hire you without a high school education. And what if you want to attend college later? Why don't you register with Hana in my class and take it from there?" Her eyes crinkled softly as she smiled. "It's your decision."

Mrs. Miller's compassionate demeanor caught Tomi off guard again. She knew Mrs. Miller's arguments were well founded, but she needed to have them validated by someone outside her inner circle. Moreover, she was relieved that she wasn't reprimanded.

Mrs. Miller gave the registration form to Tomi. She signed it while Hana stood over her with a smile tugging at the corners of her mouth.

Everyone looked toward the door as the sound of quick footsteps was heard, and the floor vibrated slightly in response. A Caucasian boy in his teens entered and greeted Mrs. Miller.

"Hi, Mom. Am I too late to help? I met some guys at the canteen and got hung up." He looked at the two girls self-consciously and shuffled his feet as he looked down at his shoes.

"You're just in time, David," responded Mrs. Miller. "I just finished enrolling the girls." She turned toward them and introduced her son. "He will be attending high school with you girls; in fact, I believe you are all in the same core class."

David Miller was a head taller than the girls. He had his mother's hair and skin coloring, but his blue-green eyes bore tiny flecks of orange. He also had his mother's easy smile, and his gangly, adolescent body reminded Tomi of a baby giraffe.

Tomi and Hana exchanged glances. Mrs. Miller read their thoughts and proceeded to explain that she and David would be living in the camp compound where he would attend high school and she would be the school advisor as well as a core teacher.

Both girls wondered if Mrs. Miller had a husband but dared not ask. They were curious to know why a Caucasian woman with a teenage son would *want* to live in an internment camp and teach.

"I know we're lacking supplies and equipment, but we'll make do," she said brightly. "By the way, if you girls know any university graduates, have them contact me. We can use them as assistant teachers to make up for the shortage of teachers."

Tomi and Hana left the classroom and hurried toward the recreation hall.

"Mrs. Miller is really nice, isn't she?" said Tomi.

"Yeah, I'm glad she talked you into staying in school."

Tomi ignored the remark. She was angry with herself for succumbing so easily to Mrs. Miller. It was not often she was given a chance to make her own decision without a confrontation. She was not sure she hadn't been hoodwinked. Instead she answered, "David is sure skinny and tall. He's all legs and arms, but he seems like a nice guy. I wonder what he thinks about being in camp."

"Gee, I don't know," replied Hana.

\* \* \*

Tomi was not overjoyed at the prospect of going back to school. She had become accustomed to roaming the camp at leisure and filling her time doing whatever she pleased. On the other hand, Hana and David eagerly relished the idea of embracing academic challenges. As time slipped by, the three became inseparable, with Tomi reluctantly tolerating the prodding of her two friends to become more intellectually stimulated.

At first, David's appearance in camp and attendance in the high school classes were met with polite silence and curiosity by the other students. But his easygoing personality abated the notoriety of a Caucasian boy among the *nisei* students. He quickly adapted to camp life and eased his way into the teenage crowd without incident.

The laundry room became their hangout. The three met there to study and socialize. Hana's radio was always blaring Glenn Miller's music and drew glares of disapproval from the *issei* women doing their laundry until she turned down the volume. There was a constant flow of traffic through the building as people arrived to do their laundry and gossip, in addition to those cutting through the building to escape the muddy road between the barracks.

David's curiosity about his new friends was perennial, and he hounded them for answers. Once he observed a small group of young men in their early 20s passing through the laundry room. Although he could not understand what they were saying, he noticed the men spoke Japanese proficiently.

"Hey, how come you girls can't speak Japanese like that?" David asked mischievously.

"Huh! 'Cuz we're not *kibei*," Tomi said smugly.

"What's that?" asked David.

"The *kibei* were born here in America, but some of them were sent back to Japan when they were pretty young and grew up like Japanese kids," said Hana.

"Why don't you like them, Tomi?" asked David.

"I don't know," Tomi's voice trailed off. "They're different. They don't act American-ish."

"I don't get it," said David. He scratched his head in mock disbelief. "What's *American-ish?*"

Hana smiled at his frustration. "She means they aren't like the *nisei*. After all, the *kibei* were educated in Japan so when they came back here, they had a hard time fitting in," she explained. "My cousin, Makoto, was there for three years. He and his *kibei* friends couldn't wait to come back from Japan, and they got here just before Pearl Harbor. Makoto said the Japanese military was taking over the country and he didn't want to be drafted in Japan."

"Actually, my older sister is a *kibei*," acknowledged Tomi. "She had been raised in Japan since she was a baby, so when she came over here she had to go to English classes. Now, she talks to me in half English and half Japanese. She's still hard to understand."

"How come I haven't met her?" asked Hana.

"She's married and lives in Block 10. We hardly see each other anymore." Tomi's thoughts turned to her sister, Yuki. She felt guilty putting her down for her poor English. Tomi vaguely remembered Yuki arriving from Japan as a painfully shy young woman in her late teens. Tomi was barely 5 at the time and could not understand why Yuki was always so withdrawn and sad. Yuki finally attended English classes, but she never became fluent enough to communicate with other *nisei*. As time went by, Yuki became more withdrawn and the bonds between the two never materialized.

\* \* \*

By the end of winter, Minidoka High School was in full swing and Hana and David eagerly joined the school activities that mush-

roomed all over the campus. Tomi stubbornly refused to partici-
pate in the mess hall dances and other social functions the school
had to offer. There were rumors floating within the camp that the
government was going to allow people to leave camp under certain
conditions. Unknown to Kiku, Tomi had gone to the Administration to inquire about a permanent leave from the camp and was
told she could apply as soon as the forms were completed. She
fueled all her energy into making plans to leave Minidoka after
graduation. She had no time for frivolous nonsense. Tomi was determined to leave and spoke incessantly about her plans to her two
friends whenever they met in the laundry room.

Hana and David began to be concerned about her obsession
and at one point Hana asked Tomi, "How are you going to make
a living?"

Tomi smiled ruefully. "I have to have a job before I leave camp,
and the only thing open are the housemaid jobs."

Hana and David looked at each other and burst into laughter.
They knew how much Tomi hated housework. Tomi had vowed
she would never make a living doing housework like her mother.
To her, it was subservient and degrading.

"You! Doing housework? laughed David. "You'll never make it."

"Oh yes I will," said Tomi stubbornly. "I'll do it if I have to."

"Have you told your mother yet?" asked Hana.

"No. Not yet. I'll tell her when I get the application."

"Oh yeah," the other two said in unison. They all knew she was
avoiding the inevitable.

# 16

## The Loyalty Questionnaire

Christmas came and went with very little celebration. It was just another cold winter's day with a fresh blanket of snow that covered Minidoka. An attempt was made to organize a mess hall decorating contest, but not many people were interested. Tomi avoided greeting her friends with the traditional Christmas wishes, which she felt were hollow and meaningless.

New Year's Day was just as ordinary, but 1943 was to usher in more demands and drastic changes for the internees. It started out with the announcement by the War Department to recruit an all-*nisei* combat team from among the men in Hawaii and the 10 internment camps on the mainland.

Tomi could not believe her eyes. She mulled over the article in the camp paper, the *Minidoka Irrigator*, which outlined the government's intention to recruit volunteers from each camp. She was waiting for Hana and David in the laundry room for a study session when she came across the article that announced a special force of Army recruitment officers coming to Minidoka.

"Volunteers will sign a loyalty questionnaire," she read. Tomi snickered in disbelief, but by the time Hana and David found her, Tomi was grim and her face betrayed her anger. She showed them the headlines.

Stunned, Hana asked, "What does all this mean?"

"I'll tell you exactly what it means," said Tomi, venting her frustration. "The Army is running out of men and they want a bunch of guys in the front lines—our guys! How stupid do they think we are?"

"Don't be silly, Tomi," David said. "The Army would never do anything like that. They don't use men as cannon fodder."

"Oh yeah? Did you read where it says these guys have to sign a loyalty questionnaire too? What do they want? Blood? Oh yeah, I forgot, they *are* asking for that too," she finished sarcastically.

"Oh, don't be like that, Tomi," admonished Hana. "I heard the JACL encouraged the government to set up an all-*nisei* volunteer unit to prove our loyalty."

"You're kidding. What's wrong with them? I'm beginning to wonder about the JACL."

"I don't know why you're so upset, Tomi," mused David. "I thought you guys wanted the *nisei* to be able to volunteer."

"That was before we found out the government keeps lying to us. Why should we believe them now?" Tomi said bitterly.

"Well, I have to admit the government says and does whatever they please," said Hana. She turned to David and explained, "After Pearl Harbor, all the *nisei* men were classified as 4C [enemy aliens] and those who were already in the Army were either kicked out or reassigned to lousy jobs like KP duties. And now, according to this article, they want the *nisei* men to volunteer for duty!"

"Wow." David gave a low whistle.

"Did you read the loyalty questions, Hana?" asked Tomi. "What do you think of them?"

"I'm confused," Hana said as she scanned the article. "Is this questionnaire only for the guys who are volunteering or what?"

"That's what so maddening. Read the darn thing. According to the paper, the questionnaire covers everyone over the age of 17, including the *issei!* Look at Questions 27 and 28. That's the kicker! It's stupid! How could our parents answer those questions without incriminating themselves?"

Hana zeroed in on Question No. 27 and read:

> *Are you willing to serve in the Armed Forces of the United States on combat duty whenever ordered?*

And for the women it read,

> *If the opportunity presents itself and you are found qualified, would you be willing to volunteer for the Army Nurse Corps or the WAAC?*

Question No. 28 read,

> *Will you swear unqualified allegiance to the United States of America and faithfully defend the United States from any or all attacks by foreign or domestic forces, and forswear any form of allegiance or obedience to the Japanese emperor, or any other foreign government, power, or organization?*

Hana sucked in her breath and let it out slowly. "I see what you mean, Tomi."

David looked puzzled. "What's wrong with the questions? Sounds okay to me."

"You can't see it, David?" asked Hana. "Question 28 says it all. It's the height of insult. How can they even ask that question of the Japanese Americans who were born in this country? Why would we say we were or were not loyal to the emperor and Japan when we were *never* involved with Japan? So, a 'yes' answer will mean we *were* disloyal and a 'no' answer means we *are* disloyal. We can't win! It's a trick question."

"Well, personally, I think you guys are getting too suspicious. All I see are a couple of questions asking you to declare your loyalty," said David.

Tomi's voice became loud and biting as she attacked David. "That's because you're a Caucasian and you're looking at the question the way you would answer it," she said irritably. "We see it as another bunch of lies."

"After all," chimed in Hana, "a year ago the *nisei* weren't good enough to serve in the Army and now all of a sudden they are. You have to admit, David, that it doesn't make much sense to expect people who have been thrown in camps to be eager to sign the questionnaire and volunteer for the Army."

David sighed and agreed, "Yeah, I see what you're talking about. I know I wouldn't want to sign up to volunteer under those circumstances."

"According to the paper, there's going to be a meeting in the mess hall tonight," said Hana. "Guess we should go and find out what's going on. I'm really confused."

"Guess so," said Tomi glumly.

David stuck his face in Tomi's and teased, "What a grouch!"

Tomi rolled up the newspaper and whacked him across the back of his head. He grabbed his head dramatically as he groaned and rolled his eyes. Tomi's mouth curled into a grin. His clowning broke the tension, and the three friends gathered their belongings and silently shuffled out of the laundry room, returning to the sanctity of their own barracks.

\* \* \*

That evening, the mess hall was filled to capacity and the noisy crowd were voicing their opinions about the questionnaire among themselves. Tomi sat with Hana at the front and saw four men huddled near the food counter. Tomi recognized Jack Mori, a staunch supporter of the JACL, and John Tani, the manager for Block 21. The other two men appeared older than the two *nisei* and didn't look familiar to her. Their faces reflected the anxiety and confusion of the crowd as they struggled to organize the meeting.

Finally, Art Myers, the administrative director of Camp Minidoka, strode into the hall. He worked under the auspices of the War Relocation Authority, or WRA, and was known for his sincerity and compassion. He was one of the few Caucasian administrators who had earned the trust and confidence of the people who were interned in Camp Minidoka. His large frame made him look much taller than his 6-foot height, and he dwarfed the other four men. Art Myers gently arched his body forward to match their height as he greeted them. His tactful gesture did not go unnoticed, and Tomi watched with approval. Aside from Ethel Miller, her core teacher, he was the only *hakujin* in camp she trusted.

The meeting started briskly with Mr. Myers articulating on the success of the War Bonds purchased by the internees in the camp, and thanking everyone for the continuation of the blood plasma drive. There was a restlessness that rippled through the crowd as he spoke.

Jack Mori thanked him politely for the platitudes and addressed the crowd. "Mr. Myers is here to clarify the interpretation of the loyalty questionnaire, which all of you have either received or read about in the camp newspaper. I have asked Mr. Zentaro Yamauchi and Mr. Kinji Hori to act as interpreters for the *issei*."

All eyes were focused on the men in the front of the mess hall. The murmur of the crowd subsided to a hushed silence. Mr. Myers cleared his throat. His voice was calm and well modulated, but Tomi detected a veil of tension masking his face.

"Let me get right to the source of contention," said Mr. Myers. "The loyalty questionnaire has raised many questions, and I am here this evening to help you discern the truth. Let me reiterate what has transpired. Initially, the questionnaire was devised to register all male *nisei* of draft age for the Selective Service. Then, the War Relocation Authority suggested incorporating the same loyalty questions for those who wanted to leave camp and who would also have to fill out an application for leave clearance. This category would include all *issei* men and women and *nisei* women who plan to leave camp." He read Question No. 27 for draft-age men as well as the version for women asking whether they would volunteer for the U.S. Armed Forces. He then read Question No. 28 asking for unqualified allegiance to the United States.

Before Mr. Myers could continue, John Tani vaulted from his seat and confronted him. "How does the WRA justify asking the *issei* the loyalty question when they were never allowed to become United States citizens as mandated by law? It cannot be answered either yes or no without serious consequences for them. My parents are *issei*. They are afraid a 'yes' answer will leave them without a country, and on the other hand, a 'no' answer will make them look disloyal. What are they supposed to do?" John raised his arms in despair. "Not only that but look at Question 27," he continued. "Does the government *really* expect an older *issei* woman to volunteer as a nurse or a WAAC?"

Art Myers shifted his weight as he closed his eyes and ran his hands through his hair in frustration.

"The department is aware of these discrepancies now, and I assure you that steps have been taken to reword the questions," said he in a firm but quiet voice.

A low rumble of discontent swept through the mess hall and subsided when Jack called for order. Tomi stirred restlessly in her seat. As the interpreters relayed Mr. Myers' message, she could hear the voices of the *issei* rising in alarm. Through their interpreters, a swift volley of questions was directed at Mr. Myers. He tried desperately to calm them, but many of the questions were being taken out of context and the issue at hand was buried under irrational fears. In the midst of the pandemonium, Tomi suddenly decided how she would answer the loyalty questions. It would be her passport out of camp.

"Where are you going?" asked Hana, as Tomi got up to leave. "You can't go yet. The meeting isn't over."

"Yeah, you're right," said Tomi with a Cheshire cat grin on her face as she sat down again.

"Okay, what are you up to now?"

"I'll tell you later."

"Uh-oh," said Hana knowingly. "I bet I know what you're going to do."

"No, you don't," Tomi shot back. For the rest of the meeting she hardly heard the frenzied exchange of questions and answers. She was in her own little world, plotting her next move.

Finally, Mr. Myers promised to follow up on the discrepancies in the questionnaire and halted the meeting. It had gone from bad to worse, and in spite of all his efforts, Art Myers could not quell their animosity. His credibility was threatened by the lack of reassurance he had to offer. The two girls left and walked together in silence as both mulled over the fiasco that had ensued that evening. Tomi's anger rose and melted into bitterness. She barely acknowledged Hana as they parted to go to their separate barracks.

She saw a dim light coming from the small window of her room in the barrack. She leaped over the two rickety stairs leading to the small landing and opened the door. George was sitting on his cot with a letter from Steve Hayama in his hand. Steve's mother, Hatsuye, and Kiku were cousins. Although the families were never close, the evacuation was the thin thread that kept them connected. They clung to the familiarity of family ties by keeping in touch through letters.

"Did Steve say anything about the loyalty questionnaire?" asked Tomi.

"Yep, he decided to answer 'no' to both questions," said George. Guys like him are called 'no-no boys.'"

"What! How could he be so dumb! Doesn't he know he'll be sent to Japan with his parents? At least they have a good reason. He doesn't know anything about Japan and hardly speaks Japanese."

"I know," said George quietly. "Worse than that, he'll be renouncing his American citizenship."

The Hayama family had been whisked to the Tule Lake camp from Minidoka because Hatsuye and her husband, Tetsuo, decided to repatriate to Japan. Tetsuo had a small hotel in Seattle, and when the evacuation order was announced, he had to sell his hotel at a great loss. After paying the bills, he had nothing left. Tetsuo knew his dreams for a better life would never be realized because he could never become a citizen or own any property. Now his son, who was an American citizen, was locked up with the family in Tule Lake, a segregation camp. For Tetsuo, repatriation was the only solution.

Tomi continued her tirade. "You know what? Steve should know it doesn't matter what the government says or does. It doesn't mean anything. Me, I'm answering 'yes' to both questions so I can leave this dump. I've decided if that's what they want to hear, then that's what they'll get."

"You talk big. You have no idea what is involved," said George in an exasperated voice. "Steve says if he is drafted or asked to volunteer for the Army, he wants the government to admit they were wrong to put us in camp."

Tomi's mouth dropped in amazement. "What a waste of time. They would never admit such a thing. He's nuts."

"He's got a point there," said George thoughtfully. "In fact, tomorrow morning I'm going to the Ad building and telling those Army recruiters what I think of them."

Tomi never thought her quiet, unassuming brother would take a stand on an issue of this magnitude. She was astounded. "Are you really going to do that? she asked. "You know you could get into a lot of trouble."

"I know."

"Did you tell Mama what you're going to do?" she asked.

"Did you tell Mama you were leaving camp?" he shot back.

A slight vibration on the wood floor warned them of someone approaching the room. Kiku entered with a small enamel basin cradled in her arm. It held her *hachi-maki* washcloth and a bar of Ivory soap. A worn, damp bath towel hung limply from her shoulders. She looked at them suspiciously and asked, "What was the meeting about? Anything important?"

"No, not really," answered Tomi. "Mr. Myers was trying to explain what the questionnaire was about but nothing was making any sense."

"Yes, I know," said Kiku in Japanese. "Many of my friends think it's a ploy to force the *issei* to leave camp and become prey to a hostile environment with no means of survival." Kiku pulled the towel over her head and as she briskly rubbed her hair, she caught Tomi and George exchanging quick glances. They turned away from her, and Kiku realized both siblings were hiding something from her.

Unknown to Tomi and George, Kiku had received a letter from her cousin, Hatsuye. Her son, Steve, had answered "no, no" on the questionnaire and she was worried sick that the government would arrest and put him in the stockade. Kiku did not share that concern with her children. She knew they had enough to contend with.

Tomi lay on her cot but was too perturbed to fall asleep. She tried to block out the mounting negative aspects of the questionnaire and wondered if she would ever get out of camp. The searchlight penetrated the cloth curtain hanging from the small window, and the silent sentry swept across the small room. Tomi finally drifted into a troubled sleep accompanied by her brother's deep breathing and her mother's soft snore.

# 17

## Indecision

When Tomi awoke the next morning, George had already left for the Administration building. She leaped out of bed and startled Kiku, who was preparing to go to the laundry room.

"Why can't you be more ladylike?" scolded her mother.

Tomi didn't answer. She dressed quickly without bothering to wash up and headed for the mess hall where she found Hana finishing her breakfast. Tomi joined her and told her about George's plan to discredit the Army recruiters.

"I sure hope he knows what he's doing," said Hana. "I'm still not sure how to answer Question 28. My parents are really disgusted with the way we've been treated by the government, and they're seriously thinking of repatriating to Japan. If they do, I'll have to go with them. I can't leave them to fend for themselves—they're too old. I don't know what to do."

"You know you could never live in Japan. You hardly speak the language, let alone know anyone over there. How would you survive?"

"I don't know, but will it be any better here?"

"It will be—it has to be," Tomi answered adamantly.

Suddenly, they heard a loud, angry voice coming from the table behind them. Tomi recognized Ichiro Kamba, a *kibei* who frequented the laundry room with his other *kibei* friends, who had all grown up in Japan. Ichiro had singled out Jack, the JACL leader who monitored the meeting the night before. The two men were face to face, straddling the bench seat that was fastened to the table where they were sitting.

"You *inu!*" Ichiro screamed, calling Jack a dog in Japanese, his face red and distorted. "How can you people in the JACL collaborate with the government and turn in your own people?"

Jack understood enough Japanese to know "inu" was a term of utter contempt and belittlement, especially from a total stranger. "Now just a minute. Can't we talk? What's your gripe?" he asked, trying to stay calm and controlled.

John, the block manager, rushed up to the two men and admonished them. "I will not tolerate any violence. We cannot afford to fight among ourselves. Now, both of you, back off! I don't want to have to call security."

Ichiro jerked his leg over the bench and gathered his utensils and plate as if to leave. He turned to Jack and snarled, "Don't ever turn your back on me because I am going to get you!" This time he spoke in English and his eyes were blazing with hate.

"Son of a bitch!" swore Jack. He threw his fist at Ichiro, but John stepped in to shove him away and blocked his blow before he made contact. John turned to Ichiro and yelled, "Get out of here! You don't even live in this block. Don't let me catch you around here again." Ichiro stormed out of the mess hall and yelled, *"Inu!"* as he slammed the door.

Until now, Tomi wasn't aware of the intense hate and resentment some of the *kibei* had built up. Most of them, like her own sister, did not hold radical views like Ichiro, and she was shocked at the extent of his anger. A low murmur spread through the hall as everyone nervously tried to gloss over the incident and ignore the uproar.

"Gads!" said Tomi. "What's his problem?"

Hana scooted closer to her and whispered, "Remember my cousin Makoto, who is a *kibei*? Well, Ichiro actually tried to get him to join the Dark Demon Club so they could go around scaring people into answering 'no, no' on the loyalty questionnaire."

"Oh, you must be kidding!" exclaimed Tomi. "People don't do things like that. Not even the other *kibei* like Ichiro. Why would they care?"

"You are so naïve sometimes!" said Hana. "I'll tell you what. Makoto has some business at the Administration building today so he'll be dropping by. I'll ask him to meet us in the laundry room at our usual place around 2 o'clock, so you can ask him yourself."

That afternoon, the three friends waited in the laundry room for Makoto to arrive. Tomi brought David up to date on what had happened in the mess hall that morning.

Finally, Makoto showed up, but he appeared apprehensive. He was a short, wiry young man in his early 20s. His thick, black hair seemed to leap from his scalp, and the huge, black-rimmed glasses dwarfed his small but pleasant features. The combination gave him a startled look. It was apparent Makoto did not want to be there, and he looked around anxiously. "What do you guys want?" he grumbled. "I can't stay long."

Hana made a quick introduction and asked him to explain Ichiro's behavior.

Makoto stood by the wooden table where everyone was sitting and began to speak reluctantly.

"When Ichiro and I were about 7 years old, both of our families moved to Japan. I came back by the time I was 13, but Ichiro and his family stayed over there until just before Pearl Harbor." Makoto shifted his weight and drummed his fingers lightly on the table. Tomi moved restlessly in her seat and wondered why he was so apprehensive. Finally, he joined them at the table and described his own argument with Ichiro about the loyalty questionnaire.

"He wanted me to answer 'no, no' to Questions 27 and 28. Worse yet, he wanted me to help him force other people like you guys to do the same," explained Makoto.

"What for?" asked David in amazement.

Makoto looked at David patiently and went on. "Before the war broke out, I was drafted into the U.S. Army. But when Pearl Harbor was bombed, the Army decided that since I was a *kibei*, I was a security risk and threw me out. That's how I ended up in camp. Can you believe they didn't trust me?" he said. Makoto shoved his hands into his pockets and absently kicked the leg of the table as he shook his head in disbelief.

"So when I heard the Army was asking for volunteers, I decided to reenlist as an interpreter in the Military Intelligence Service. I have something to prove. I am not a traitor. But Ichiro wants me to get back at the Army by stirring up trouble just for the hell of it. Wait until he finds out I'm reenlisting!"

"Ye gads," muttered Tomi under her breath. Tomi was not sympathetic to Makoto's flag-raising patriotism. It sounded superficial and self-serving. She could not understand either man's point of view and dismissed Makoto's ramblings as insignificant and Ichiro as a fanatic nuisance.

Makoto looked at his watch. "Well, I gotta go. My appointment is in half an hour." He spoke briskly as he turned from the table and walked away.

"Is he really going to sign up for the MIS?" asked David.

"I guess so," said Hana, shrugging her shoulders.

The trio was left with a sense of emptiness. The issues concerning the loyalty questions were becoming more confusing. They sat there for a long time without talking.

David broke the silence. "I don't think I would reenlist if I were in Makoto's shoes."

"I *know* I wouldn't," said Tomi emphatically while Hana sat without commenting. They left the laundry room while the muffled sound of gossiping women reverberated and the sound of sloshing water echoed in the damp building. David decided to head for the canteen while the girls headed for Tomi's barrack.

Tomi wondered if George had returned from the Ad building and how he had fared with the Army recruitment officers.

"Let's go see if George is back yet and find out what happened," said Tomi. "Hope he's not in too much trouble."

"Maybe I shouldn't go in," said Hana as they approached the barrack where Tomi lived.

Their voices awakened George, who had been napping. He yawned and sat up stretching his arms over his head. The book he had been reading tumbled to the floor.

"Well, what happened?" asked Tomi eagerly.

"Nothing," said George, but his voice had an edge to it and betrayed his disquieting state of mind. George looked straight at her. "I volunteered for the Army."

Tomi gasped, "You did *what?* You're joking, right?" She heard the door close quietly behind her and knew Hana had tactfully left before a confrontation erupted.

"You heard me," said George. "I decided to join the Army."

"But that's not what you said you were going to do," accused Tomi. "What changed your mind?"

George took his time answering. He ran his fingers through his thick wavy hair and dropped his chin forward on his chest. Finally he looked up at Tomi and said, "I had a long talk with the recruiting officer and he convinced me that the *nisei* can prove their loyalty by volunteering to enlist in the Army. He told me there are a bunch of politicians who are preparing legislation to take away our citizenship and ship us to Japan along with the *issei* after the war. If we refuse to fight in the Army now, they'll use that as another excuse to ship us out. What choice do I have?"

"Do you believe that?" exclaimed Tomi. "Sounds like he was threatening you. Anyway, it doesn't matter. The government will do what they want to."

"No, he wasn't threatening me," said George patiently. "He was just telling me some of the reasons why I should volunteer. That happens to be one of them."

Deep inside, Tomi knew George was right, but resentment and bitterness seethed within her, leaving her with a feeling of utter contempt toward her brother.

"For crying out loud! I don't understand you!" Tomi screamed at him and stomped out of the barrack. She wandered through the laundry room and curled up on the bench against the tar-papered wall. She felt betrayed by her own brother, and yet she knew he really did not have any choice.

Tomi huddled on the bench and watched the string of people passing through the laundry room. Her sanctuary was invaded by a parade of chattering women, who stood at the sink to gossip as they washed their clothes on the scrub board. Soon darkness fell, and someone finally switched on the light. Tomi continued to sit there until she heard Hana's voice asking, "Want to go eat? They're clanging the dinner bell."

"Sure, why not," answered Tomi. She unwound herself and slowly got off the bench. They sloshed through the mud in silence and quickened their pace as they linked their arms together and joined the crowd in the mess hall.

Hana did not question Tomi about George's decision to enlist, nor did Tomi offer any information. Both girls were numbed by the series of events that had taken place in the last few days and chose not to discuss it.

They waited patiently in line and scooped some rice and over-boiled wieners mixed with cabbage onto their plates. Although the quality of food had improved with time, today was not one of them.

"Ugh," said Tomi. "Wieners again!"

"Well it's better than eating *tsukemono* [pickled vegetables] and rice every day like we used to," said Hana as she chased the swollen wiener on her plate and stabbed it with a fork.

By the time dinner was over, Tomi decided to declare a truce with George. She was still not in favor of him volunteering for the Army, but she was grateful that he wasn't creating any trouble like the "no-no boys" in Tule Lake. Tomi left Hana in the mess hall and walked back to her barrack where she found George playing solitaire on his cot. He looked up as she stood next to him. "I guess you know what you're doing," she said and walked over to her cot and sat down.

George grinned wryly and replied, "I hope so." That was his way of accepting her awkward attempt to apologize for her outburst.

That evening, George approached Kiku hesitantly as she sat on her cot mending her clothes.

"Mama," he said nervously. "You know I went to talk to the recruitment officer today. Well, I joined the Army and will be leaving as soon as I pass the physical."

Kiku did not look up from her work and her face showed no emotion. Her nimble fingers guided the needle without missing a stitch.

"Are you sure this is what you want to do, George?" she asked calmly.

"Yes, Mama," he answered in a determined voice and explained to her why he had decided to volunteer and what the recruitment officer had said. He spoke to her slowly in broken Japanese, struggling to use the correct words.

Kiku put down her sewing and looked at her son. She sighed and said, "You know you will have to go to your father and tell him what you have done."

"I will go to his barrack and talk to him tomorrow."

Tomi was surprised at her mother's quiet acceptance of George's pending departure. She expected a storm of arguments even though she had always felt that her mother favored George over her.

But Kiku's calm reaction gave Tomi the courage to divulge her own plans to leave camp. She took a deep breath and her words tumbled out in torrents. "Mama, I have something to tell you too. After I graduate from high school, I am leaving camp. I have already applied for a leave clearance and want to leave as soon as I can."

Kiku looked shocked. Her body stiffened and her head snapped toward Tomi. The cot squeaked loudly as she stood up to confront her daughter. "What do you mean you are leaving camp?" she demanded. "How are you going to support yourself? What a foolish girl you are!" Kiku stormed. Her voice quivered as she glared at Tomi and she whispered loudly, *"Baka!" Stupid!* Kiku felt helpless as she realized her control over both George and Tomi had slipped away in one fell swoop. It seemed as if her whole world had come crashing down on her yet again.

Tomi cringed at her mother's onslaught and closed her eyes as if to ward off her attack. She realized too late that her announcement was ill-timed. She had become the recipient of her mother's frustration and anger.

George's voice cut through the tension and Tomi heard him say, "Let her go, Mama. She will be better off outside camp. Can't you see what camp life is doing to everyone? People are beginning to fight among themselves and the kids are doing whatever they want. There is no future for her here. She has to leave." He spoke to his mother in English, but she understood every word.

Tomi opened her eyes and stole a glance at her mother. Kiku had resumed her stoic mask.

"Perhaps you are right, George." She turned to Tomi and said in a cutting voice, "I hope you have thought this out wisely. You are no longer a child and the future is in your own hands. You must go to your father and tell him what you are about to do and get his permission." Kiku turned away and resumed her sewing.

Tomi could hear the ringing in her ears accelerate as it always did whenever she was upset. It drowned out the dead silence that permeated the small room.

# 18

## Papa's Blessing

The next day Tomi trudged up the long, dusty road to find her father's barrack. She had not seen or heard from him since he and George had the confrontation last spring in Camp Harmony. All she knew was that he was living in the bachelor's quarters in Block 12, Barrack 22A. She was still chafing from her mother's tongue-lashing the night before and was not looking forward to her father's usual tyrannical behavior. She remembered how he used to terrorize the family. Tomi was the only one who escaped his ire because she was the youngest and could run under the bed the fastest. There would be no beds to hide under today, she thought ruefully.

Tomi found her father's barrack and even before she knocked on the door, she could hear the muffled sound of male voices. Tomi knocked timidly, and the door opened to reveal a roomful of men. Some were playing poker on a wooden table covered with an old Army blanket, and others were lying on their cots napping or reading a book. It looked like a huge men's dormitory.

"Who are you looking for?" asked the young man who opened the door.

"Does Mr. Saburo Inouye live here?" she asked shyly.

"Oi! Saburo, someone to see you!" he yelled.

"He's over there," said another man, jerking his head toward the back of the building. Tomi thanked them both and worked her way through the maze of cots and spotted her father sitting on a crudely made chair reading a book. He looked out of place among all the young bachelors. Saburo lowered his head slightly to look over the frame of his glasses. He saw his daughter and acknowledged her with a nod.

"What do you want?" he asked gently.

Tomi told her father her plans to leave camp. She chose her words carefully so as not to repeat the mistake that she made with her mother. Saburo studied the pages of his book intently and, without looking up, said, "If this is what you want to do, you should do it." Tomi's heart leaped with joy. She could not believe her father was giving her his blessing. She was elated.

"Do you have any money?" asked Saburo.

"No, Papa, but the government will give me train fare to wherever I find a job and $25," she answered.

Saburo frowned and thumbed through the book. "It won't be easy living on the outside. How will you survive?"

Tomi spoke haltingly in broken Japanese and English. "I have to apply for a job before they let me out of camp. There are plenty of jobs for house girls, but I can find something better once I am out. I can do it, Papa," she said eagerly. "Anyway, I heard the local farmers are short of help, and the government will be allowing us to go work on the sugar beet farms this spring and summer. I will sign up for sugar beeting and earn some money," she said lamely, not sure of how her father would react.

"Very well," said Saburo. "You must do what you think is best."

He looked at Tomi, trying not to reveal his concern for his youngest child. She stood there, uncomfortably shifting from one foot to the other. It was not often her father approved her requests without an argument. He silently dismissed her by dropping his gaze and pretended to resume his reading as if she were not there.

"I will let you know when I get my clearance to leave, Papa," promised Tomi.

Saburo shifted in his chair and crossed his legs as he kept his eyes on the book. "Mmm, you do that," he murmured.

Tomi flew down the hill on winged feet. For once she was not subjected to her father's outbursts. She realized it was a rare moment in which he had really listened and heard what she said without flying into a rage. She could hardly wait to tell George how their father had changed.

George listened to Tomi in disbelief as she told him about her talk with their father. Past experience had taught him to approach Saburo with caution. He had been deliberately putting off his visit with Saburo to avoid the inevitable clash.

The next morning George reluctantly walked up the hill to his father's barrack where Saburo greeted him in the same manner as he had greeted Tomi. George wasted no time in stating his intention to enlist in the Army and was startled by his father's quiet approval and passive demeanor. George stood with his eyes riveted on Saburo's face, expecting him to erupt into a tirade at any moment. A long, uncomfortable silence marked their fragile bond, which had teetered precariously for years.

Finally, as George turned to leave, Saburo slowly got out of his chair and placed his hands on his son's shoulders. "Be brave and strong. *Shikkari, yo!*" he said in Japanese. Then he turned and walked away.

George was baffled by his father's change in attitude toward him. Even as a sickly little boy he had sensed his father's disappointment in him. Saburo's show of support today was as close to any sign of approval as he had ever shown George. Nonetheless, it was a bittersweet moment for George. He was aware that many of his friends' parents were opposed to their sons volunteering for the

Army. They considered the evacuation a travesty of justice and had lost faith in the system. The continuous violations of their trust had left a bad taste in their mouths. Parents were not willing to sacrifice their sons to a losing proposition.

How ironic that his father had chosen to support him now on such an explosive issue. George felt comforted by his father's unexpected approval and found peace within himself that he had volunteered for the United States Army.

# 19

## Hash and Rehash

It was almost spring, but winter lingered longer than expected. Everyone was bundled up, hoping for warmer weather to arrive. Finally, during the first week of March, George received his orders from the Army to report to Camp Shelby in Mississippi.

Tomi, meanwhile, was alarmed to hear that four hoodlums had attacked Reverend Noda of the First Baptist Church last week. They accused him of encouraging the young men to volunteer. Everyone knew Reverend Noda's only intention was to counsel and comfort the men who came to him for advice, and nothing else. So the brutal attack was considered a cowardly act and a disgrace to the camp community. On the other hand, many families were hopelessly divided in their views about enlisting. There were endless arguments between parents and sons that split the families apart. Tomi herself was feeling guilty for resenting her brother's decision to enlist, and she tried to make his last few days in camp as pleasant as possible.

The evening before George was to leave, two of his buddies came by to wish him well. There was no fanfare or celebration, but instead, a solicitous mood hovered over the group. George, who was a loner, never had many friends but had met Joe and Yosh in the mess hall where they worked.

"Did you hear about the draft resisters?" asked Yosh, trying to make small talk.

"Yeah," Joe chimed in. "A bunch of *nisei* in Heart Mountain formed a group called the 'Fair Play Committee.' They feel that the government was wrong to put us *nisei* in camps and equally wrong to expect us to serve in the Army when our constitutional rights have been taken away."

"Ahh, those guys know damn well the government isn't going to listen to them," Yosh said. "They ought to stop making trouble for the rest of us. No one outside the camp is going to back them. And they sure aren't going to get the support inside the camp either. It's a crazy scheme—they'll probably all land in jail. Besides, a lot of those guys don't even want to go to war."

"Are you calling them cowards?" gasped Tomi.

"Hey, hold on," intervened George. "Just because those guys don't want to be drafted or to volunteer doesn't make them cowards. After all, I wasn't going to volunteer either for the same reasons, but I changed my mind."

"How come?" asked Yosh.

"We all know this internment is not legal," George spoke slowly. He wanted to make sure Joe and Yosh did not misunderstand him. "The government could care less about our civil rights. You guys know that the *hakujins* don't even think we are their equal. So what makes you think they'll consider the Bill of Rights as something we are entitled to?" he asked. "The only way to convince the government that we're loyal is to show them we're willing to fight for our country."

"Hah, you sound like a politician," smirked Tomi.

"Shut up!" snapped George.

Yosh and Joe grinned as the two bantered back and forth.

"What about you guys? What do you think is the right thing to do?" asked Tomi.

"All I know is what my friend wrote to me from Tule Lake," said Joe, avoiding her question. "He says over 60 guys are involved in that Fair Play Committee fiasco. The administration at Heart Mountain is really worried that more *nisei* will join, so they arrested the whole group and threw them in the stockade. On top of that, all the 'no-no boys' and troublemakers like Ichiro are being sent to Tule Lake."

Tomi knew what Joe said was true. Hatsue had written that Tule Lake was considered a maximum-security segregation center. The original internees in Tule Lake who were not disloyal resented the arrival of the dissidents that swelled their population to 3,000 more than the center could accommodate.

"I may not even answer the loyalty questionnaire," Yosh said.

"That'll be the same as being a 'no-no boy,'" said George.

"I don't like being accused of being loyal to the Japanese emperor. That's the way the questionnaire reads." Yosh's voice was getting loud. "I am not a Japanese!"

The three men moved about restlessly in the small room until George suggested going outside to the back of the barrack to continue their discussion.

A few minutes later, Tomi peeked out the window and saw them huddled up against the side of the barrack. They were sitting on their haunches and she could hear their muffled voices arguing. Eventually, George came back and she knew by the look on his face that the parting was not amicable.

Kiku sat on the edge of her cot and tended to her mending as usual. Occasionally, she would steal side glances at her son as he tried to read. Tomorrow George would be leaving Minidoka for Camp Shelby. Yet she said nothing to him to convey her fears about his safety and welfare.

When Kiku left the room to go to the latrine, Tomi sidled up to George and said, "I hear the Army is looking for *nisei* girls to volunteer for the WAAC [Women's Army Auxiliary Corps]. What do you think of me enlisting instead of leaving and finding a job out east?"

George bolted straight up from his cot. "What! Are you out of your mind?" he yelled.

"Gee whiz," said Tomi, taken aback, "I didn't say I was going to join...I was just asking what you thought. How come you're so upset?"

"Never mind," said George. "Just stick to your original plan and leave camp like you said you would."

Tomi was puzzled by George's reaction, but she was secretly glad that he was so concerned. It made her feel as if she was finally connecting with him as a sibling.

"Anyway, those WAAC uniforms are really ugly," said Tomi flippantly. "Did you see those awful shoes?"

George cussed under his breath and flung himself on the cot. "...As if I didn't have enough to worry about," he muttered. Tomi had a wide grin on her face as she turned away from him and left the room, slamming the door behind her.

The next morning after breakfast in the mess hall, Tomi and George walked up the dusty road with Kiku lagging behind as they all headed for the main gate. When they approached the top of the hill, they could see small clusters of people gathered at the gate, where two armed guards were standing, with two others in the guard station. This would be the last time George trudged up the dusty road. He was trading his life in camp for a new career at Camp Shelby as a soldier. The underlying mood of the people standing there was gloomy, but emotions were kept in check. On the surface, it appeared to be a casual send-off, not a life-altering journey, for six young people leaving home. George was the only Army volunteer leaving camp that morning. Tomi surmised that the other five were leaving to go back east for jobs.

It was a lonely send-off for George with only Kiku and Tomi to wish him well. Saburo was nowhere in sight. The guards conducted a final check, and it was time to go. Before George boarded the bus, Kiku hesitantly touched his arm and said, *"Ki o tsukenasai, ne."* *Please be careful.* He nodded silently.

"Don't forget to write to me," said Tomi brightly.

"Yeah, sure," George said gruffly.

The bus left in a cloud of dust, causing everyone to cough and sneeze. As it picked up speed, the bus turned into a swirling tunnel that rolled across the plain. Soon, all Tomi could see was a small white puff that finally disappeared.

Tomi and Kiku walked down the hill together in silence to their room. John, the block manager, was already at their door to pick up the extra cot. He apologized profusely while he broke down the cot and made a hasty retreat out the door. Tomi pulled down the old sheet that separated the room. At least with George gone she wouldn't have to change her clothes under the blankets anymore or scoot sideways to get out of the room.

# 20

## The Letter

Kiku heard the rustle of paper as mail was shoved into the crude box hanging outside their room. She opened the door and retrieved it. Her eyes caught an envelope addressed to her from Cousin Hatsuye, and she quickly opened the letter. Somehow the letter escaped the usual censor and was delivered to Kiku in its entirety.

Hatsuye had dispensed with the usual formal greetings and started the letter with the shocking news of her 17-year-old son, Steve, having been wounded by military police during a riot at Tule Lake. The letter was written in Japanese with deep sadness and went on to describe what happened:

> It all started when a gang of radical kibei beat up a JACL leader who was suspected of being an informer, and they almost killed him. In the meantime, Mr. Takeno, who is the head of the Kitchen Workers Union, was arrested as a suspect. However, it is a well-known fact in camp that he had evidence on Mr. Cogswell, the warehouse supervisor, who was stealing the rationed sugar and running a black

*market outside the camp. Everyone felt the arrest was a*
*cover-up for Cogswell.*

*A mass meeting was held to protest the arrest. Mr. Takeno's*
*supporters knew he was not the attacker and wanted him*
*released. Attempts were made by the camp leaders to dis-*
*perse the crowd, but communication broke down and the*
*mob headed toward the jail to continue their protest. At*
*the same time, the radical kibeis decided to go after more*
*JACL informers and were roaming the camp looking for*
*other victims.*

*According to Steve, he and his friend Jimmy were walk-*
*ing toward the Administration building when they saw the*
*noisy crowd heading up the hill. Totally unaware of the*
*impending disaster, they were swept up in the crowd.*

*At the top of the hill they saw three military guards lined*
*up with shotguns. The guards ordered them to disperse*
*and lobbed tear gas into the crowd. Steve and Jim turned*
*and started to run down the hill, but it was too late. The*
*guards started to shoot and both boys were caught in the*
*line of fire. Steve was not badly hurt, but his friend Jimmy*
*was shot in the back and died instantly. He was only 18*
*years old. I cannot believe someone so young had to die so*
*needlessly. I heard there was another death, but I am not*
*sure who it was. At least eight other people were shot and*
*are still in the hospital.*

The letter ended abruptly, with promises of an update on the
volatile atmosphere at Tule Lake.

Kiku translated the letter to Tomi, who felt disheartened. The
shooting triggered emotions about her brother that she had sup-

pressed. It made her uneasy to think that George would soon be facing enemy fire on a daily basis and might not come back. She quickly dismissed the thought by rationalizing he would be safe within the protection of his Army regiment. It won't be like Tule Lake, she surmised. She withdrew into the safety of her imaginary cocoon to insulate herself from reality.

Kiku was spent. She was thankful that Minidoka had very few uprisings and radical dissidents compared with Tule Lake. Her heart went out to her cousin, who had to endure such trauma, but she herself had just sent her only son to fight for a country that demanded 100% loyalty with nothing in return. And she knew he might not come back. Her cousin almost lost a son in a different way. These were dangerous times—a reality both women had to live with. Kiku folded the letter carefully and slipped it back into the envelope. The future was bleak, but there was nothing to do but *gaman*.

# 21

## City Girl

Tomi's determination to leave camp intensified. Her whole being was centered on the day she could leave Minidoka, but she needed money. The train fare and a check for $25 as promised by the government would not be enough to sustain her. When she heard about the opportunity to work on a local farm, she seized it. With the war in full swing, there was a labor shortage and the farmers petitioned the local government to help recruit seasonal farm help because they were in danger of losing their crops. What a great way to earn extra money, thought Tomi. She remembered going to a farm when she was 12 to pick berries and what fun it was to pick and eat them at the same time. Surely harvesting sugar beets could not be that much more strenuous. She looked up her friend, Fudge Kitano, who was raised on a farm, to ask her about it.

"Ahh, it's not that hard," Fudge had said. "All you have to do is cut the top off the sugar beet and load it on the truck."

Fudge, who was 18 years old, did not look like a farm girl. She was a classic beauty. Her flawless features were reminiscent of a Japanese porcelain doll, and her petite figure was perfectly proportioned. She was aware of the admiring glances of young men and often expressed annoyance at her father, who discouraged any of them from dating her. Tomi, who grew up as a tomboy, felt awkward and clumsy whenever she stood next to Fudge but secretly admired her elegant femininity. It didn't take Fudge long to persuade Tomi to sign up for sugar beeting along with Fudge's younger sister, Mitzi, and several other friends. Tomi was sure if someone who looked as fragile as Fudge could do farm work, she, the tomboy, could certainly handle it.

"My father will be with us, and he'll show you how to top and load the sugar beets," Fudge promised.

Mr. Kitano was a strict father, but he was also a quiet, patient man. The first day on the farm, he worked alongside Tomi and made sure she knew how to handle the long knife that curved slightly on the end. He showed her how to pull up a sugar beet with the knife and chop off the leafy top. She could not emulate his precise and rhythmic movements. However, by the end of the day, Tomi could top the beet without chopping half of it off. She was frustrated with her inability to keep up with Fudge and the other girls as they threw the topped beets in a neat roll. Mr. Kitano murmured encouragement to her from time to time as he kept a watchful eye on his daughters and the other girls. By the end of the day, Tomi was thoroughly wilted. She had never been so tired in all her life. She ruefully wondered what made her think she could keep up with her friends, who were used to the back-breaking labor.

After supper, Tomi flopped on her bed and could hardly keep her eyes open. She was exhausted and every muscle in her body was aching. She could hear the muffled voices and chattering of her friends in waves of broken sounds, and finally she drifted into a deep sleep, oblivious to her surroundings.

\* \* \*

The following day, Tomi tried hard to keep up with her friends, but her whole body protested and her arms felt like lead. A large, slow-moving truck kept pace with the workers as they topped and loaded the sugar beets. She saw John Fisher, the farmer, on top of the wide-bed truck. He wore blue coveralls and a wide-brimmed hat that teetered on the back of his head. He was an easygoing man and well liked by the workers. John was shoving and piling up the beets to make more room on the truck. Tomi cinched a sugar beet with her knife and topped it. Without looking, she gave the beet a mighty heave and sent it flying. She heard a thud and a low grunt. She had smacked John right on the mouth, and the force threw him backward on top of the sugar beets.

Tomi stood rooted in place with her mouth open, and she dropped her knife. Mr. Kitano ran quickly to the truck and helped John down.

Tomi gathered enough courage to approach the farmer as he wiped a small trail of blood off his chin with his dusty handkerchief. "I am sorry," she said in a small voice. "I wasn't looking when I threw the sugar beet...." Her voice trailed off, and John mumbled something as he continued to dab at his mouth. He reached over and patted her shoulder gently and waved her away. She could not hear what he said, but she was relieved to see he was not angry at her. At that moment she felt that no amount of money was worth the agony she was suffering.

The men worked on the other side of the field and could be seen working fast and furiously as they kept pace with the moving truck. One late afternoon, she and the girls noticed John's wife making her way through the field where the men were working. She was struggling with a huge tray balanced in both hands.

"I wonder what she's doing?" Fudge said under her breath. All the girls stopped their work to see what was going on.

They could hear the echo of the men's voices whooping and hollering and someone yelled, "Oh boy! Cake and ice cream!" The distance between the fields was at least half a mile apart, but the girls could make out snatches of words as the men hollered to each other in glee.

Tomi's usual quiet indignation gave way to open anger. She threw up her hands and said loudly, "Well, that's not fair! We work hard too. How come we never get cake and ice cream?"

John, who was standing close by, heard her but did not say anything. He looked at her with a wry smile and walked away.

\* \* \*

The next day Lucy Fisher brought a tray of cake and ice cream to the girls. *"Now* are you happy?" asked John with a grin. It was a hollow victory for Tomi, and somehow, it didn't feel right. She wondered why she felt so guilty for speaking out. Nonetheless, there was some consolation in relishing the special treat.

Mercifully, the sugar beet season was almost over. Tomi was amazed to find that she was looking forward to returning to camp—and getting away from farming.

# 22

## Freedom

Tomi was excited. It was almost time for graduation and she had already applied for clearance to leave Minidoka six months ago. It would only be a matter of time before she was free. The thought of leaving camp sent her mind reeling with exhilaration and apprehension. Graduation was not a priority for her until Hana reminded her of the upcoming prom and commencement ceremony.

Tomi didn't care about going to the prom. She had no particular ties with the senior class and was content to chum around with her small group of friends. Hana, on the other hand, was more sociable and eager to join all the festivities. She coaxed Tomi to go with her to the canteen to look through the Sears catalog and order a dress for graduation. Finally, Hana chose a pink, rayon dress with a Peter Pan collar and long sleeves. It had a row of tiny white buttons in the front above a v-shaped waistline and full skirt. She fussed about the price but in the end decided to pay the exorbitant cost of $4.50. Tomi's choice was a simple white cotton waffle dress with a square neck, short sleeves and a slightly flared, belted skirt for $2.59.

After they placed their orders at the canteen, Tomi and Hana walked down the hill, gleefully anticipating the arrival of their dresses. They stopped at Tomi's barrack, and Kiku handed Tomi a thick, official-looking envelope.

"What is it?" asked Kiku, eyeing the letter suspiciously.

"It's from the WRA," answered Tomi as she tore open the letter. "They want more records and signatures from the school to complete the clearance forms before I leave camp even though I already answered four pages of questions."

"On what?" asked Hana.

"Same old thing—my loyalty to America," she sighed. "On top of that, I had to give them five personal references, and they wanted the letters to come from Caucasians if possible."

Kiku was sitting on her cot sorting out George's clothes. Tomi looked over at her mother and for a fleeting moment she felt guilty for being elated about the prospect of leaving camp. For the time being, her mother seemed to have adjusted to camp life and never expressed a desire to leave. But she knew it would be difficult for both of them to survive without money in an unknown environment. In the past year, the daily crises had become a way of life and Tomi dealt with them in succession. Now, there was no time to prioritize; there was much to do and little time.

Tomi and Hana rushed out the door and headed for the school barracks. Tomi shuffled through the official forms as they walked, and she came across copies of the letters of reference submitted by her teachers and employers in Seattle. She steered Hana to their hangout in the laundry room to read the letters and was stunned to find that only two of the five letters confirmed her loyalty and proof of her Americanization.

The first letter was from Mr. Levy, who denied ever knowing Tomi. The next letter was from Mrs. Hill, who claimed the length of Tomi's employment with her as a babysitter was too short to make an assessment. The third and most crushing blow came from her home room teacher, Miss Sidney, whom she had counted on for support. Miss Sidney stated she could not fairly appraise Tomi's loyalty because she had never met her parents or was in her home. The letter ended with a curt affirmation that read, "However, it would seem that any Japanese student applying for a pass would know that until she proved her loyalty, she would be closely supervised and would make a supreme effort to justify that trust." Tomi reread the letter and realized Miss Sidney was just protecting herself and had distanced herself from Tomi. The one person she relied on had failed her, and she was devastated. She and Hana pored over the letter in disbelief. The two girls sat in the damp laundry room in silence for a while, not knowing how to cope with the betrayal.

The fourth letter was from Kay Connor, her English teacher, who wrote a concise and firm affirmation of Tomi's loyalty. She ended her letter by stating, "I believe her loyalty and patriotism cannot be questioned."

Finally, it was the last letter that took the sting out of Tomi's disappointment. Mrs. Marguerite Howard wrote a compassionate, in-depth letter about Tomi's good qualities and loyalty, without any concern for herself or fear of repercussion from the government. A couple of summers ago, Tomi had spent six weeks with her as a "mother's helper" in Bothell, Washington, and it was evident that Mrs. Howard considered her more than an employee. She ended her letter by acknowledging Tomi as a friend and said that she wanted to get in touch with her. Her letter was a salve for Tomi's wounded spirit and the key to freedom.

Hana looked worried and asked Tomi if she felt two references were going to be enough to satisfy the WRA. Tomi shrugged and answered, "I can't worry about that now. I've come this far. Besides, I know a few other people who will vouch for me." Her bravado did not match the uneasy feeling in the pit of her stomach. She was unwilling to accept the possibility of not being able to leave Minidoka. Tomi gathered up the letters and the two girls retraced their steps to the school barracks to get the required signatures for the clearance papers.

* * *

Graduation time was a blur of activities. The high school that was hastily assembled in the mess hall less than a year ago had flourished into a school with a full staff, books, supplies and classrooms. The first graduating class of Minidoka High School had survived the transition and was rewarded with all the amenities, including a senior banquet and prom in the mess hall and a graduation ceremony with blue caps and gowns in the half-built amphitheater.

The dresses that Tomi and Hana ordered from the Sears catalog arrived a week before graduation. Other than the hem and the cuff on her sleeves that needed shortening, Hana's dress fit perfectly. Tomi marveled at how the pale pink color of the dress complemented Hana's fair skin. On the other hand, Tomi's dress was far too large for her. The dress drooped over her small frame and the comical effect sent the two girls into a fit of laughter. The neckline gaped and the waistline floated around her hips. Hana's mother, who was an expert seamstress, offered to alter the dress for Tomi. The result was nothing short of a miracle. The white cotton dress sculpted her petite figure perfectly. Tomi could not believe it was the same dress and wore it with gratitude and pride. To top it off, her mother was somehow able to rustle up a pair of beige silk stockings. In spite of herself, Tomi had to admit dressing up was exhilarating, and she allowed herself to relax and fully enjoy all of the graduation events with her classmates.

* * *

It's about time, Tomi thought to herself. Her application to leave Minidoka had finally been approved, and she gripped the clearance letter tightly. It had finally come through, but all she could feel was irritation and a strong sense of urgency to expedite the process. The only thing left for her to do was to apply for a job anywhere in the east. Tomi's skills were limited to babysitting and light housekeeping, and she knew her choice of jobs would be limited. She finally settled on a position as a "domestic helper" offered by the Rosenberg family in Toledo, Ohio. The pay was $13 a week with one week's vacation after one year of employment. Tomi had no intention of staying with the Rosenbergs any longer than she had to. Her plan was to save enough money to move to Chicago, where jobs were plentiful and paid better.

Tomi suppressed her excitement and uncertainty as the day of departure neared. She nervously packed and unpacked her battered suitcase. At one point, one of Kiku's friends, Mrs. Ohara, had come over for a visit and watched Tomi go through her packing ritual. She said in Japanese, "Tomiko-san, you have made a big decision to leave camp like a mature woman, but on the other hand, you act like a child who doesn't know what to do."

Tomi said nothing but smiled weakly in response. She resented Mrs. Ohara's perceptive observation but was not deterred by her unkind remark.

Tomi was surprised to get a letter from the WRA informing her that Fumi Higa, who lived in Block 24, had also accepted a job as a domestic helper in Toledo. Fumi was an acquaintance, who was a couple of years older than Tomi, but she was unlike most *nisei* girls. Her affable personality instantly drew people to her, and her genuine openness and caring nature were a refreshing contrast to the guarded nature of their peers. Tomi wasted little time in looking up Fumi, who welcomed her with open arms. Together, they compared notes about their pending employment in Toledo. They spent many days exchanging thoughts about the future and both agreed that their jobs in Toledo would be a stepping-stone to Chicago. Gradually the gap that stemmed from the difference in their ages faded away, and Tomi felt secure in their budding friendship. Fumi was clearly someone she could depend on in a pinch. Both she and her mother were relieved that someone as reliable as Fumi would be a familiar figure in the uncertain future.

Hana and David continued to support and help Tomi as she made preparations to leave. They teased her unmercifully about her career as a domestic helper, but their concern for Tomi's welfare became their primary interest. Their last day together in the laundry room was tense. There was no big fanfare or farewell party. It seemed out of place to celebrate, considering the circumstances and the uncertainties. The three kept their emotions light and reminisced about their time together until Security Police broke up their session.

The day finally arrived for Tomi's departure from Minidoka. A few of Kiku's friends dropped by to give Tomi a card with a dollar or two enclosed and their good wishes.

Hana and David came over early, and the three walked up the hill together for the last time as they headed for the main gate. Once again, Kiku lagged behind, allowing Tomi and her friends more time together. She looked for her father, but Saburo was nowhere in sight. Tomi had visited him a week ago to let him know she was leaving, and he responded by giving her a long lecture on family pride and *giri* (sense of duty) that her mother had already pounded into her. He gave her $15 for emergencies, and cautioned, *"Ki o tsukenasai,"* (Be careful), and turned away. She had hoped that he would come to see her off.

Kiku held herself in check as Tomi playfully bantered with Hana and David. Tomi handed Hana a small envelope and said, "Open this after I get on the bus. And don't laugh, okay? It's something I wrote. Hope you don't think it's corny."

"What about me?" asked David.

"You can read it too."

She turned to her mother with a mixture of excitement and sadness. Kiku tried to straighten Tomi's hair as the summer breeze swirled around them. She tugged at Tomi's coat and ran her hands gently around her collar and said, "Be sure you let me know when you get to your destination. Be careful. And *gaman yo*." There was much to say in the little time they had together. Her hands dropped to her sides and she stepped back to gaze at her daughter for the last time.

"Yes, Mama. I will write you as soon as I get to Toledo," she promised.

It was time to go. The guard opened the barbed-wire gate and Tomi got on the bus with her suitcase. She could hear the chorus of "goodbyes" as the half-filled bus took off in a cloud of dust.

The guard closed the gate and everyone moved away from the fence to escape the dust kicked up by the departing bus. Hana opened the envelope and found a poem that Tomi had written:

> *My soul no longer cries in vain*
> *No longer feels the pain*
> *The road to nowhere has no gate*
> *It has no key or chain.*
> *I will ride the clouds and*
> *Chase the stars,*
> *Until I find my name.*

Tomi was free.

## About the Author

After leaving Minidoka Relocation Center in Idaho, Toshiko Shoji Ito journeyed to Toledo, Ohio, where she worked as a house girl. She later moved to the south side of Chicago, and her parents joined her after being released from Minidoka. She worked in a variety of positions and received a beautician's license in 1948. Soon after, Toshiko married Dave Ito, who had been in Company G, 442$^{nd}$ Regimental Combat Team. In 1956, the Itos drove from Illinois to California and settled there with their two sons and a daughter.

In 1973, Toshiko joined the staff at Citrus Community College in Azusa, California. She received her bachelor's and master's degrees in education and became head of the cosmetology department at Citrus.

Retirement has slowed the pace of Toshiko's professional life but new projects and volunteer work now fill her time. This is her first novel.